ABRUPTLY SEVEN WAS SHOVED FORWARD . . .

. . . by one of the Klingon sentries who had finished scanning her. "This one is clean," he snarled at Lursa. Spittle hung off his lower lip as he eyed the sisters.

Seven assessed the situation, particularly Lursa's enraged eyes. Thrusting her foot backward, Seven caught the hairy sentry in his belly. Even though she was barefoot, the blow was effective because the sentry was unprepared, undoubtedly preoccupied by his desire to join the melee below. Her heel sank in deep, and then his chin was wide-open for her double-fisted swipe. He was unconscious before he hit the floor with a resounding boom.

That was one she wouldn't have to deal with on her way out.

Seven instantly dropped her guard, letting the others know she wasn't in a fighting mood. There was silence for a moment, with the sentries warily looking from her to their downed comrade.

Lursa's expression lit up, while B'Etor chortled at the prone form. "Rotten sack of *veQ!*" the younger sister taunted, kicking his leg aside as she passed by.

Lursa narrowed her eyes at the sentries to keep them in line, then gestured sharply for Seven to move along. Seven complied.

STAR TREK®

BOOK
DARK PASSIONS
ONE

SUSAN WRIGHT

POCKET BOOKS

New York   London   Toronto   Sydney   Singapore

An *Original* Publication of POCKET BOOKS

POCKET BOOKS, a division of Simon & Schuster, Inc.
1230 Avenue of the Americas, New York, NY 10020

STAR TREK is a Registered Trademark of Paramount Pictures.

This book is published by Pocket Books, a division of Simon & Schuster, Inc., under exclusive license from Paramount Pictures.

ISBN: 0-671-78785-3

First Pocket Books printing January 2001

10 9 8 7 6 5 4 3 2 1

POCKET and colophon are registered trademarks of Simon & Schuster, Inc.

Printed in the U.S.A.

Acknowledgment

Kudos to John Ordover for his brilliant idea to feature the powerful women of *Star Trek* in a novel set in the Mirror Universe.

The setting for *Star Trek: Dark Passions* Books One and Two is the dark, intense "Mirror Universe" as established on *Star Trek: Deep Space Nine,* and reflects the lifestyles and mores of that universe. The players are not the Star Trek characters as we have come to know them, but their harder, crueler, alternate universe equivalents.

The date is sometime before Major Kira and Dr. Bashir rediscovered this harsh realm where humans are enslaved by a Klingon, Cardassian and Bajoran alliance; where no one knows whom to trust.

Chapter 1

ANNIKA HANSEN, AGENT Seven of Corps Nine for the
Obsidian Order, waited patiently for her quarry to appear. Agent Seven had been undercover on Khitomer for
several days, having been surgically altered to appear as
a female Klingon warrior by the physicians of the Cardassian intelligence agency.

The other females in the Khitomer communal house
accepted Seven's story that she had jumped ship to
avoid her captain's wrath over a shipment of isolinear
coprocessors that had gone astray. She claimed she was
now trying to earn her passage back to Qo'nos, the Klingon Homeworld.

In the dark recesses of the hall, Agent Seven lightly
scratched the Klingon ridges on her forehead. As part of
her disguise, her hair had been lengthened, frizzed, and
colored dark brown. The traditional female armor covered every part of her body except her chest, leaving her

vulnerable to a knife attack in the finest Klingon tradition. To defend herself, she had spiked boots and gloves, and her three-bladed *d'k tahg,* honed razor sharp.

Agent Seven's current mission had come straight from Enabran Tain. She was ordered to assassinate Duras, son of Ja'rod. The intelligence brief Tain had downloaded into her cranial implant database had included the fact that Duras frequented this particular establishment whenever he was on Khitomer.

Seven's decision to infiltrate this communal house had paid off. For the past three evenings, the Duras sisters had visited the house looking for a woman to keep company with Duras. Tonight, Seven had no intention of allowing them to leave without her. Her orders from Tain were clear. She must complete the assassination before the Cardassian delegation arrived on Khitomer for the Alliance gathering. Then she had to withdraw from Klingon territory without being detected.

A fine mist covered Khitomer, drifting through the open spaces between the slanting black columns of the communal house. Seven was in the base of the pyramidal building, whose upper levels were lined by rows of tiny square windows. The first two floors were open, forming an atrium on a wide stone terrace. Iron lamps hanging from the high ceiling gave off a fuzzy glow that barely penetrated the darkness. When the clouds rose from the moist ground, Seven could see the cliffs of the nearby mountains. Usually visibility was near zero.

Agent Seven leaned against a slanted column next to the entryway preferred by the Duras sisters. Other Klingon women were drifting down from their rooms on the upper floors to lounge on the benches scattered throughout the atrium. Since Khitomer was in close proximity to the Romulan front, these were fierce women, battle scarred and ready for action.

Seven's tight leather gloves, doubly thick to hide her slender fingers, reminded her of her first Klingon simulation at the Obsidian Order training facility. That experience had gone on for weeks as she attempted to complete her assignment—assassinating a Klingon official called Gorloth, son of Poq.

Maybe she was thinking of that first training simulation because of its similarities to this assignment. Then she had posed as an available Klingon woman in the darker side of town, attempting to draw Gorloth's attention and maneuver him into a position where she could kill him.

But the training simulation seemed very far away, and Seven had to think hard to remember that although she had been playing a Klingon seductress, she had actually just entered puberty. She had been scared that she wouldn't succeed and her trainers would punish her. It made her bold and daring, despite the seemingly real surroundings.

It was a valid fear, because sometimes the training simulations turned out to be real. Seven remembered questioning everything during that first assignment. She hadn't been in space in years, not since she was six years old on her parents' ship before it crashed on a deep-space Cardassian colony. She had spent the entire time wondering: Is this ship really moving? Are those stars real? Is this pilot an Obsidian Order agent, a hologram of one, or a real pirate? Time she should have spent getting into character had been wasted.

Other trainees often argued over whether the Obsidian Order surprised them with real assignments because they were needed for the job, or because the uncertainty kept them on constant alert. It was true that trainees came and went, casualties in the line of duty. Seven never grew close to any other trainee. They were shifted from one undercover character to the next, complete with physical and psychological modifications. Even when they were in group training situations, they didn't recognize one another.

Seven had failed her first assignment, and luckily it had been a simulation. But a few subsequent sessions had turned out to be real. Her training had been thorough, and now it was second nature to slip into her required cover. Seven had become Melka, daughter of Kagh. Her real self lay tightly curled inside the Klingon shell, watching her own actions with analytical detachment as she bared her teeth at a towering female, hissing slightly to force her away from the choice spot by the entry columns.

Agent Seven knew she was good because she had received her orders directly from Enabran Tain. Tain had seen her worth when she was only a child and had accepted her into the Obsidian Order. With her parents dead, Annika Hansen had first been adopted into a high-ranking Cardassian family. Yet despite a physique altered to make her appear Cardassian, the Ghemor family could not fully accept a Terran as a daughter. After only one year, Ghemor had sent her to the Obsidian Order, making it clear that the Terran slave camps were her only option if she failed again.

The mist parted from the entryway as the Duras sisters appeared. Lursa was matronly despite her unmarried state, with a perpetually sour expression. Pretty B'Etor stayed close behind her elder sister's shoulder, forever in her shadow. They scanned the hall; Lursa's mouth puckered in distaste. B'Etor peered enviously around her sister, perhaps desiring the freedom of these warriors.

Seven stayed back for a moment as Lursa imperiously rejected the first women who approached. Duras had a reputation for being a passionate and honorable Klingon, one of the few men who had earned the respect of the communal women. However, it would lower the family's status if Lursa took the first offers she received.

When Lursa hesitated and began to inspect one female with serious intent, Seven made her move. With several long strides, her hand poised on the *d'k tahg* at her waist, Seven reached the Duras sisters. Catching them by surprise, Seven thrust the fawning communal woman aside.

Seven spit after her. "Duras, son of Ja'rod, deserves better than a mewling kitten!"

"Who tells *us* what our brother deserves?" Lursa demanded contemptuously.

"I am Melka, daughter of Kagh," Seven replied, loud enough for the entire hall to hear. "But any woman here would tell you the same. Duras, son of Ja'rod, deserves only the best."

Lursa was eyeing Seven with new interest. "Are *you* the best?"

Seven laughed, showing off her pointed teeth. "I leave *that* for you to decide."

Lursa and B'Etor examined her as Seven stood with her hand on the knife. It was like acting in a holoplay. Inwardly, her eyes were rolling at the overdone gestures and ritual displays of dominance. Yet Seven flawlessly executed the behavior best designed to obtain compliance, sorting instantaneously through the suggestions her cranial implant whispered directly to her mind.

Now her undercover work paid off. The communal women had learned to respect her and none dared to challenge her, even with Duras as the prize. Lursa looked from Seven to the women huddled back in the wan glow of the lamps.

"It grows late," B'Etor murmured.

Lursa abruptly raised her hand, cutting off her sister. "I don't like her."

Seven shrugged. "If you think I am too aggressive for Duras, then choose another."

Hissing laughter echoed off the stone columns as the communal women acknowledged Seven's direct hit. If Lursa had been a stronger woman, she would have struck Seven where she stood. But the Duras sisters were fundamentally weak. Seven had recognized that fact the first night they came to the communal house.

"You dare—" B'Etor started to exclaim. Lursa blocked her sister as if holding her back.

Seven's sneer conveyed her contempt. B'Etor was not offering a serious challenge. The soft laughter continued.

"You will learn your mistake," Lursa told Seven. "Come!"

Seven didn't show unseemly pleasure, knowing that Lursa could change her mind if she did not act properly grateful. Seven didn't care about Klingon power games. All she needed was a few moments alone with Duras, and her mission would be completed.

The Duras family had come to Khitomer for the upcoming Alliance gathering, to prepare the city for the arrival of the Regent and the Klingon delegation. According to Seven's intelligence information, Duras had taken command of an empty building at the edge of the city. The danger from the nearby Romulan front was evident to Seven as the flyer taking her to Duras passed low over huge impact craters that collected mist, remnants of previous attacks on the planet. But the Klingons had never lost Khitomer.

Seven was certain that Khitomer had been chosen for the Alliance gathering because it served as a reminder of the vast border of space ravaged by the ongoing Romulan war. However, the data on this matter was limited, so she concentrated on the task at hand.

The Duras standard had been boldly painted on the roof of the structure—a blatant sign of his presence. The standard was like a clenched fist raised to the overcast sky: Duras was telling Romulan kamikazes that he did not fear their laser strikes.

Effective, yet predictable, in Seven's opinion. She readied herself with the bio-mental techniques that would enable her to maximize her performance.

The Duras sisters escorted Seven down the stairs from the roof pad and into a scanning booth. Seven mentally detached herself from the routine of the sentry interrogation and the interior and exterior scans. She used her trained mind to shut down the cranial implant so the enhancements in her brain remained cloaked. She had no worries that her DNA would reveal her true heritage. For this assignment, the Obsidian Order's surgical unit had attached a genetic Klingon tag to her chromosomes. It would take a level-1 diagnostic, lasting several hours, to detect her enhancements. Most scans were merely a level-3.

Her cover personality, Melka, answered the Duras sentries exactly as a sullen Klingon spaceworker would. She also fought the removal of her knife, boots, and spiked gloves as any decent Klingon would. Apparently Duras had been badly cut up during his encounter last night, and the sentries joked that he wanted some entertainment that wouldn't require hours in the regeneration unit. The Regent, Worf, son of Mogh, was arriving tomorrow morning.

Meanwhile, loud Klingon voices and laughter echoed up the spiral stairwell, along with the clash of metal and the rumbling thump of wooden objects being smashed. The Duras entourage was celebrating before the gathering that would be attended by the ruling empires of the Alliance.

During Seven's stay in the communal house, she had heard rumors that big changes were coming. For many years, there had been grumbling that the Intendants who ruled the numerous systems in the former Terran Empire were mismanaging trade matters for their own gain. At the last session of the Klingon High Council, Duras had proposed that a special position be created to oversee trade in the Alliance territories. The most likely candidate for such a powerful position was Duras himself, Worf's closest ally on the Council. Duras traditionally backed Worf against the senseless demands of High Chancellor K'mpec.

Agent Seven had been amused by the women's simpleminded analysis from a purely Klingon-centric point of view. The other powers in the Alliance would have a great deal to say about whether an Overseer's post would be created and who would be in charge. The Cardassian opinion was that the Klingons already had too much power with the Regent's position held by Worf. And surely the Tholian, Breen, and Ferengi empires would have something to say about it as well, not to mention the Intendants themselves.

Soon the matter would be decided, with the leaders of the Alliance converging on Khitomer from distant parts of the Alpha Quadrant. They were coming to a meeting that had a single agenda item—reorganizing Alliance control over trade in the fallen Terran Empire.

Abruptly Seven was shoved forward by one of the Klingon sentries who had finished scanning her. "This one is clean," he snarled at Lursa. Spittle hung off his lower lip as he eyed the sisters.

Seven assessed the situation, particularly Lursa's enraged eyes. Thrusting her foot backward, Seven caught the hairy sentry in his belly. Even though she was barefoot, the blow was effective because the sentry was unprepared, undoubtedly preoccupied by his desire to join the melee below. Her heel sank in deep, and then his chin was wide-open for her double-fisted swipe. He was unconscious before he hit the floor with a resounding boom.

That was one she wouldn't have to deal with on her way out.

Seven instantly dropped her guard, letting the others know she wasn't in a fighting mood. There was silence for a moment, with the sentries warily looking from her to their downed comrade.

Lursa's expression lit up, while B'Etor chortled at the prone form. "Rotten sack of *veQ!*" the younger sister taunted, kicking his leg aside as she passed by.

Lursa narrowed her eyes at the sentries to keep them in line, then gestured sharply for Seven to move along. Seven complied.

While waiting in a room draped in pungent leather from the walls to the vast cushioned bed, Agent Seven checked for alternate ways out. It was a long climb up the outer wall to the flyer pad on the roof, but that appeared to be preferable to confronting the sentries on the stairs.

Stripped of her weapons—*d'k tahg,* boots and spiked gloves—Seven nevertheless felt fully prepared. She readied herself, remaining firmly in the Melka character in case she was being covertly observed. She drank bloodwine, she belched, she lay sideways on the bed kicking one foot in the air as if she had nothing better to do than daydream. The sounds of raucous merriment continued on the floors below.

Finally the door swung open and Duras arrived with a puff of musky incense. His color was high, and he was grinning as if still laughing at a joke. "Begone!" he shouted over his shoulder to Klingons in the hallway. The heavy wooden door shut, muffling the noise outside.

"A drink!" Duras ordered.

Seven raised one side of her lip, watching him as she stalked toward the decanter. Duras was a handsome Klingon, in the prime of life. Pouring the wine slowly, she gave him time to come closer. He was curious now, and she averted her face, listening to him.

"They say you are a wildcat," Duras told her. "Lursa intends that I teach you your place."

Seven looked up at him, crooking her finger to beckon him closer. Duras leaned over, his nostrils flaring and the pupils of his eyes growing larger with desire.

"I know my place," she whispered, touching his chin with her fingers.

Before he could react, her other hand was on top of his head, and with a quick and practiced jerk, she snapped his neck. He knew this was the end, and tensed at the perfect moment, his eyes widening in surprise.

Duras fell hard, and she landed partly underneath him. His breath left his body and didn't return.

Seven trusted that no one would think the sounds were suspicious, or notice the thump of Duras's boots hitting the floorboards as she rolled him off her. She took his *d'k tahg*, sticking it through her waistband.

Dusting off her hands, she went to the window and opened it. During her earlier reconnaissance, she had noted that no guards patrolled the grounds of the estate. Apparently Duras employed a security ground shield to keep anyone from entering or leaving the compound on foot. So she would have to take a different route.

The climb up to the roof took more time than Seven had anticipated. The crumbling stone offered uncertain hand- and toeholds. It was also slippery from the moisture-rich air. She longed for her boots and gloves, taken by the sentries. Her fingertips, cut by razor-sharp flakes of rock, began to bleed.

With nearly two body lengths to go to the roof, Seven grew light-headed and thought she was going to fall. For a moment, she panicked.

She couldn't fail . . .

Suddenly she felt a wave of coolness wash through her. "Ahh . . ." she breathed. Her body felt lighter, her muscles stronger. When she moved, the pain that shot through her tortured fingers became a ripple of pure ecstasy.

Her cranial implant had been reactivated by the agony she was experiencing. Only elite agents of the Obsidian Order received this feature of the cranial implant. It helped them resist torture if captured by the enemy. Agents who had the implant usually died with their secrets intact.

With every heartbeat, Seven felt better. The constant waves of euphoria made her feel as though she could fly to the roof if necessary. She resumed climbing.

The hulking shadows of several flyers loomed in the mist, but there appeared to be no sentries on the roof pad. She could hear them inside the sentry hut, where it sounded like a party was taking place. Seven chose the flyer nearest the edge of the roof and crawled underneath to disable its running lights. It was an older model, and she accessed the command code directly from the onboard computer by inputting a virus that overrode security protocols.

The flyer lifted silently from the roof pad. She nudged the bar and let the flyer slide over the edge of the structure. With the afterburners ready to engage if she was detected, the flyer sank down the wall.

Using the mist as cover, she got away. It was only a matter of a few moments before she passed through the outer alarm shield, raising the alert. But she engaged the afterburners, and the flyer was off at full speed. She never saw her pursuers.

Seven proceeded directly to the busy spaceport. The Duras sentries followed, but they merely believed that a flyer had been stolen, probably by a drunken participant at the party. Surely it would take more time before it was discovered that Duras was dead. Then the full might of the Duras family would fall on the spaceport, perhaps even managing to disrupt this frantic place.

The spaceport was the only entryway to Khitomer, and each soldier who arrived on shore leave from the Romulan front passed through. Bars, restaurants, entertainment centers, and gaming establishments filled every nook and cranny, even hanging off the shaking walkways high in the air. Hordes of motley vendors and service providers in gay, skimpy costumes dotted the sea of dark leather armor. The sound was deafening.

Added to the mix were the delegations arriving for the Alliance gathering. A number of short Ktarians managed to cut a swath through the milling crowd. Their staffs let off sparkling blue jolts whenever a drunken Klingon staggered into their path. Alliance security were trying to get the Ktarian delegation through the spaceport without starting a riot.

Seven deliberately scaled several ramps and took two fast-walks to reach her storage unit. It was a midsize locker, approximately the length and breadth of her outstretched arm.

Paying the fee and opening the door, she noted the small sphere still rested inside. Holding it in her hand, she glanced around to see if anyone was watching. There were people everywhere, but nobody was paying any attention.

Seven quickly slipped inside the locker. There was a warning posted on the wall that the door would lock from the outside, but she knew she could use the power cell of the sphere to activate the latch. Last time she had hired a bed in the transit domicile in order to transform herself from a Trill into a Klingon. But now she didn't have time. Though it was cramped inside the locker, she expanded the plates of the transformation sphere, opening one end until it was big enough to fit over her head.

She quickly set the sphere for Andorian, having seen the distinctive blue antennae among the spaceport crowd. Their contingent must have arrived recently, followed by the usual throng of sycophants and merchants who served the elite Andorians. Since she didn't have much time before the Duras family would descend on the spaceport, she set the timer for the shortest sequence possible. The transformation sphere stated a warning that physical damage was possible under such conditions.

Agent Seven ignored the warning and activated the sphere. It was a good thing the endorphins stimulated by the cranial implant were coursing through her body, or she would have screamed as the sphere began lasering off her Klingon disguise. Then it applied blue Andorian skin and bleached the pigment from her hair.

It was a chop-job and probably wouldn't fool a real Andorian, but it would be good enough for her to get through the spaceport customs and pass the exit checks when she left Klingon territory. The transformation sphere could do only the most minimal adjustment to her DNA, adding an Andorian tag to the Klingon tag. If she was scanned, even with a level-3 unit, it was possible the odd mixture would be discovered. But she didn't plan to allow herself to be scanned again.

When she removed the sphere a short while later, her face felt raw, but the mirror showed beautiful sky-blue skin. The stout antennae were numb and fleshy. She brushed her short white hair into place over her eyes.

The next step was her hands, since the Klingon sentries has taken her gloves. Her fingertips were mangled, but she stuck them into the sphere. This time she couldn't ignore the pain that seared through her arms as the sensitive neurons of her hands fired and misfired from the stimulation.

Letting the sphere fall away, she saw that her hands were blue and appeared unharmed, while inside they throbbed with an intensity that rivaled the pain in her face. Each finger felt twice its normal size. With difficulty, she changed into the plain gray jumper that she had stashed inside the locker. It was the kind of suit almost any alien could wear, and now that she was disguised as an Andorian, she would blend in perfectly. She stuffed her Klingon armor into the bag to take with her. She wouldn't leave any evidence behind on Khitomer.

Now Agent Seven was ready to go.

Jadzia almost refused her entry, but Seven supplied the proper countersign. As Seven rolled open the airlock to the tiny starship *Rogue Star,* Jadzia was there to greet her. The Trill's spots appeared darker than usual against her flushed skin, as if she had been indulging in the conveniences available at the Khitomer spaceport. Yet the blade of the curved knife at her waist was polished, indicating she should not be treated lightly.

"Nice outfit," Jadzia drawled.

"Thank you." Seven had hired the irrepressible mercenary captain to transport her to Khitomer, then wait at the spaceport. Jadzia had served her well on several important missions, though she had no idea that Seven worked for the Obsidian Order.

Jadzia slyly added, "She leaves a Trill and comes back an Andorian . . ."

Jadzia's curiosity was one reason Seven hadn't returned to the ship as Melka. Reports would soon fill the Alliance about the death of Duras at the hands of a mysterious Klingon woman. The less Jadzia connected her with the event, the better. That was also why Seven had transformed herself originally from Klingon to Trill for the journey to Khitomer. She needed the pilot to handle the ship while she was undercover because the spaceport was known to "appropriate" vacant vessels in dock. The demands of the front often overrode private ownership.

"It is time to depart," Seven told Jadzia.

"So soon?" Jadzia said facetiously. She didn't seem too bothered by her wait at the spaceport. "I found the best places in this joint—"

"You will obtain clearance for departure immediately." Seven started for her quarters in the rear of the small ship.

"Who shall I say I have on board this time?" Jadzia called after her.

Agent Seven turned. "I will supply you with the proper information."

"You're the boss." Jadzia's laughter followed her into the back. "What I wouldn't give to see what you really look like . . ."

Chapter 2

REGENT WORF WAS pleased when lesser starships scattered as the *Negh'Var,* his colossal flagship, entered orbit around Khitomer. Such respect was due him as Regent of the Alliance territories. Worf commanded the Alliance armada and maintained order among the empires and colonies of the fallen Terran Empire.

A Klingon battleship scuttled away from the *Negh'Var,* dwarfed by the protruding bulbous bow of his flagship. Worf grunted in satisfaction, his chin propped in his fist as he slouched in the command chair. His warriors flew the *Negh'Var* as if they didn't care who they ran over.

"Get me the port officer!" Worf demanded of the *QumpIn,* his first officer. The *Negh'Var,* at 1400 meters long, would not dock at any of the orbital stations. Worf preferred to remain mobile while they were close to the Romulan front. Nor did he trust the other

Alliance members who were gathering on Khitomer.

"Officer Torax on screen," announced First Officer Koloth.

A bald Klingon appeared, bowing before the Regent. The port officer was scrawny, with dark overhanging brows and a long, thin mustache drooping from the corners of his mouth. *"Greetings, Regent Worf, on behalf of Khitomer. You are cleared to maintain your current orbital altitude. You may beam down to the spaceport at your convenience."*

Koloth reported to Worf, "Coordinates received."

Worf waved a negligent hand at Torax. "Tell Duras to wait at the beamdown point."

The port official started to say something, then swallowed hard. *"Uhh . . . My Regent . . ."*

Worf impatiently kicked one heel of his reinforced boot against the command chair. "Speak, you spineless *'Iwghargh!"*

"Haven't you heard? I thought—" At Worf's warning growl, Torax hastily finished, *"Duras, son of Ja'rod, is dead."*

Worf stood up, thrusting aside an approaching aide. "What! You lie!"

Torax flushed darker, making several knife scars stand out on his bald head. *"The Duras family should have contacted you. It happened last night—"*

Worf glared at Torax, who stopped with a gulp. Worf was sure there must be some mistake, and this measly officer would pay for it.

"End communication," Worf ordered. "Get me Duras!"

* * *

In the confusion that followed, Worf heard the same story, this time amplified by more unbelievable details. Duras had been killed in his own chambers, his neck broken as if he had offered himself up as a sacrificial *chun*.

Even the Regent couldn't bypass the security barrier around Khitomer and transport directly to the temporary Duras residence, so Worf beamed down to the spaceport with his aide and senior officers, leaving the *QumpIn* in charge of the *Negh'Var*. The reactions of those at the spaceport confirmed the reports. The ravening hordes actually paused to watch him march by, following his every move as if assessing what this death would do to the Regency.

Worf bared his teeth, knowing his hair stood on end. His pointed toes flashed their razor-sharp spikes with every stride. No one questioned him! He clenched his fists in his metal gloves, wanting to lash out at the curious eyes, pleased whenever he saw fear reflected there.

Duras had come early to Khitomer to prepare for Worf's arrival. The planet had been volatile since the legendary Khitomer massacre, when Romulans had killed over four thousand Klingons . . . including Worf's family. When the first Klingon ship had arrived after the destruction, Duras's father Ja'rod had taken custody of the young boy Worf. Worf had been adopted into the Ja'rod family and had grown up with Duras as his brother. They had fought together, served together, and plotted to take over the Klingon Empire together after Ja'rod was killed in a skirmish with a Romulan bird-of-prey.

Worf had objected to Khitomer as the site of the Alliance gathering, but Duras had convinced him that it would remind everyone of the real enemy—the Romulan Empire.

"This way to your flyer—" the port official started to say.

Worf smacked him across the face without breaking stride and left the spaceport. Whoever had killed Duras would die a terrible death.

Tradition decreed that the body of the slain could not be moved until it was taken away for disposal. The way a warrior died was mirrored in the death posture, and the manner of death would determine a warrior's fate in the afterlife.

Worf stepped into the bedchamber, which was lit by a single lamp. A mounded form darkened the floor.

Members of the Duras family and entourage huddled in the doorway. Worf had left his own people on the roof landing pad. No need for everyone to witness Duras's dishonor.

For dishonor it was. His friend's eyes were wide-open, his mouth contorted in abject surprise. He lay on his side, his legs tangled and his head bent sharply sideways. Not a knife wound or a speck of blood on him, except for the trickle from his mouth where he had bitten his own tongue in the death spasm. Killed where he stood, with a full flagon of bloodwine on the table next to him.

Now Worf could believe it. Duras was dead. Life had been taken not only from Duras, but from Worf and the

Duras family and the entire Klingon Empire. Everything that Duras could have accomplished lay on this filthy floor. A bag of empty flesh, useless and pitiable.

Worf went down on one knee next to Duras. He stared into his friend's eye, prying it open wider with his fingers, feeling the cold dead weight.

A mighty roar welled up in his throat, a howl of fury over the irreplaceable loss. It drained every breath in his body, gaining volume and scrubbing his throat raw.

But it was not the victorious exaltation it should have been. It was not the howl of warning for the dead in *Sto-Vo-Kor* to beware, a Klingon warrior was arriving. This ignoble death would send Duras down to face the *Fek'lhr* who guarded the underworld of *Gre'thor*. Duras was condemned to fight his way into hell, and if vanquished again, would wander forever as a lost wraith. But Duras would not be beaten again, of that Worf was certain.

Worf turned away from the body. He would win a glorious victory in Duras's name. Then Duras could cross the river of blood and enter *Sto-Vo-Kor*. Worf would not rest until that happened.

His eyes searched the watching retainers until he found Lursa, the eldest living Duras. Now she was the head of the Duras family.

"Tell me what happened," Worf demanded.

There was no celebration in the Duras residence. Only a warrior who died honorably in battle was celebrated as a freed spirit. Instead, the Duras family gathered with Worf in the Great Hall, the retainers glumly sitting or sprawling along the walls, their revelry abruptly ended, their future uncertain. The air was filled with heavy, cloying incense, intended to expel demons drawn by the death.

The command chair of the patriarch was left empty by tacit agreement. Lursa seemed incapable of filling it.

"As you saw," Lursa explained. "There was an open window where the female escaped. The stolen flyer was found at the spaceport. We found blood on the flyer and the outer walls. The genetic sequence is Klingon but has not been matched with any house."

As Worf paced up and down the hall, he clasped his gloved hands behind his back to keep from shaking his fist in her face. "Let me see who did this."

Lursa provided several images of the Klingon female, full face and turning to snarl at something. Worf burned the face into his mind, the slant of her teeth, the flare of her nose. He would never forget her. He would track her down and kill her himself.

Lursa said bitterly, "We are interrogating the women of the communal house now."

B'Etor shook her head in confusion. "How could a Klingon kill so dishonorably? She must be an alien in disguise."

"The sentry scans confirmed she is a Klingon female," Lursa snapped at her sister, trying to regain control.

When they were growing up together, Worf had considered Lursa ineffectual and unattractive, unlike her sister B'Etor. B'Etor had enjoyed sparring with him and Duras as a little girl, even though she lost every time. Duras had been determined to keep his sisters with him, protecting them until he could find the right family to form an alliance with. Now it was too late, and he could see that knowledge in B'Etor's eyes as she tried to get closer to him, wondering who would take her as a mate now. From a powerful clan, the Duras family had suddenly crumbled. Duras had only illegitimate sons, none of whom were ready to assume command of the family.

"Get me the scans of the female," Worf demanded. "And the security logs." He would leave no micron unturned to discover who was responsible.

"As you wish." Lursa gestured to one of the warriors, who hurried out of the hall.

Worf was not ready to blame anyone until he had proof, but he did not doubt that the upcoming Alliance gathering had something to do with this. Unlike the naive B'Etor, Worf could easily believe a number of warriors on the Klingon High Council were capable of eliminating such a powerful foe as Duras. Of the two dozen members, there was one most likely suspect—Gowron.

Gowron had opposed Worf on several notable occasions, and he had recently received a mark of favor from K'mpec, High Chancellor of the High Council. K'mpec was losing strength and was far past his prime, so speculation was running strong about who would replace the old warrior. Gowron and Duras had claimed equal-sized factions . . . until today. If this was Gowron's doing, then he was unfit to sit on the High Council.

"Would you have some warm bloodwine?" Lursa asked.

Worf ground his teeth, remembering the flagon upstairs, full to the brim and shimmering with every footfall. Not a drop on the surface of the table. Duras had not fought his death.

"Get me those scans," he ordered curtly.

By the time Worf beamed up to his flagship with the scans and security logs, he was thoroughly disgusted with the Duras sisters. Despite his objections, they had followed him back to the spaceport, trying to get in a few more words with him before he returned to the *Negh'Var.* Finally Lursa blurted out that she wanted Worf to endorse her confirmation as head of the Duras family and support her claim for her brother's seat on the High Council.

Worf was in no mood for amateur politics. The vast Duras holdings undoubtedly qualified the family to sit on the High Council, but Lursa's abilities as a leader were untested. It would be difficult for her to gain the necessary votes from the other members. However, Worf needed every vote of support on the High Council that he could obtain, and he reluctantly agreed to endorse her. Lursa was absurdly grateful. He quickly escaped her annoying presence.

Snarling at every spaceport official and the transporter operators, Worf finally returned to the *Negh'Var.* His own crew fled at the sight of his lowering brows and bared teeth.

Entering his private quarters, his aide Grelda took his cloak and helped peel off his metal-lined gloves. "Begone!" Worf ordered. The aide hurried away without a word.

Snatching his *bat'leth* from the wall, Worf swung the curved double blade through the air. "Uhhghh!" he grunted, envisioning the female who had killed Duras. He could almost see her head splitting in two, her body bleeding.

Moving through the spacious main chamber, Worf wielded the deadly *bat'leth* in a series of sweeping thrusts and feints that were an extension of his superb reach. He would have sparred with his aide, but at that moment he knew he would kill anyone who fought him.

Turning, he moved back through the chamber, sweat flying off his brow and his breath growing short. "Arrgh!" he growled, slicing through a cushion with two quick swipes, leaving a puff of silicon in the air.

But it was unsatisfying, even demeaning. Duras's death, the way he had died, being back on Khitomer again . . .

Worf glanced at the door leading to Deanna Troi's quarters. It was shut.

Surely Deanna had heard the news of Duras's death. She held a finger on the pulse of every person on board this great warship.

Breathing heavily, Worf moved closer to the door, gripping the *bat'leth* in one hand.

The door slid open at his approach, and Worf silently entered Deanna's quarters. The lights were warm and low, and there was a soothing scent in the air. He drew in a deep breath, wanting to rid himself of the fumes of sickly sweet incense that still permeated his clothing and clung to his hair.

Deanna's quarters seemed even more comfortable than his own, with clusters of inviting couches cushioned in dark, vibrant colors. Arms and armor hung from the walls and screens, much like in his quarters. But Deanna displayed pieces that were works of art, alien antiques that were intricately crafted of rare metals and studded with jewels.

Deanna appeared in the archway to her bedroom. Her Klingon armor and leggings were formal and severe, with the breastplate bared. Her dark hair curled down her back, wild and tangled, as he preferred it.

As she looked at him from across the room, Worf knew that she had heard about Duras. In one glance, he understood that she had given him privacy, waiting until he sought her out.

Deanna went to the wall and removed her favorite Cisterian saber from its place of honor. A strong flare of light caught the recurved blade as she placed the weapon in the corner. "For the *bat'leth*," she told him, gesturing to the empty pegs.

Worf went over and placed his *bat'leth* on the pegs. As usual, with her empathic sense, she had given him exactly what he needed. Not like those annoying Duras sisters, chattering over things that were only important in their narrow lives.

Staring at the *bat'leth*, he remembered that its worn brown grips had been wrapped by Duras himself. Worf wanted to tell Deanna about his friend's death, how only a beast of burden should die with its neck broken. But he could not speak, his rage was still too strong.

"Khitomer . . . ," Deanna said thoughtfully. "It is a place of destiny for you."

Surprised, Worf did not react in fury. He would have if she had mentioned Duras. Maybe it was her accent, lilting and reassuring, unlike the shrill, harsh voice of Lursa. It calmed him.

"Khitomer," Worf murmured in agreement. The last time he had been to this planet was to visit a newly erected shrine to honor the memories of the slain warriors who had fought at the Khitomer massacre. The Romulans had overwhelmed the outpost, but the Klingons had held the planet long enough for the Romulans to be caught by arriving reinforcements. Worf's parents had fought the Romulans and lost. His baby brother Kurn had been killed in the massacre that followed. Of all the Klingons who had been on Khitomer, only Worf had survived.

"You never told me what happened during the attack," Deanna said.

Worf glanced at her dark, impenetrable eyes. Only he was reflected back.

"I was on my *lur'kha*," Worf admitted. "When a Klingon child is old enough to hold a blade, he is considered a man. We are sent into the night with our blade. Only the ones who are destined to be warriors survive."

"So you survived," Deanna said.

"I saw nothing that night," Worf said roughly. "I was in the deep forest, fending off wild beasts. I knew nothing until I returned to the outpost and found the Klingons had retaken it from the Romulans. Everything was destroyed."

"But you survived," Deanna whispered.

He glared at her. Only she could bear his intensity and turn it away from herself. Deanna knew exactly what he was feeling.

She twined her arms around his neck. *"You* are a warrior."

"Yes!" Worf suddenly tightened his arms around her. "And I will destroy the *nuch* who did this to Duras! I swear it."

Chapter 3

THE CARDASSIAN *GALOR*-CLASS starship cut through space, gleaming dark gold in the light of the distant stars. The Cardassian contingent was en route to Khitomer on board the *Groumall*.

Enabran Tain, head of the Obsidian Order, the Cardassian intelligence agency, usually preferred to avoid space travel. But the Khitomer talks were a unique situation that required his presence.

Tain had requested quarters without a portal, but of course, Gul Dukat had given him a guest suite that had several of the few portals cut into the armored hull. At one time, Tain used to enjoy traveling through the starscape. He had spent several decades on ships and bases working as an undercover agent for the Obsidian Order. Then he had been chosen to become an administrator for the Order. In subsequent years, he had been conditioned to stay within the confines of the bunkers deep beneath the surface of Cardassia Prime. Tain had raised a family in the underground chambers, and had watched his daughter's marriage via computer screen, much to his former wife's dismay.

At this time, late in his career, Tain hadn't left the bunker for nearly two years. But this voyage was necessary. The question of whether to appoint an Overseer of trade in the Alliance territory was of paramount importance. It also gave him the opportunity to observe Gul Dukat for a few weeks. Dukat was increasingly troublesome.

Meanwhile, Tain tried to ignore the portals and the constant thrum of the powerful warship, unnerving after the perfect silence of his bunker.

Finally a signal announced the communications hail he had been expecting. Tain opened a return subspace channel through his personal encryption node. Contact with his agents was secured from outside surveillance, including that of Gul Dukat's crew on the starship.

A blue Andorian face appeared on the screen. Tain would have recognized Agent Seven in any disguise. For her part, Seven would see his down-turned mouth and heavy gray-green jowls, the ridges grown lumpy and thick with age. Tain had never altered his relatively small eye-ridge, knowing that it made him look forbidding and mean. Instead, he took advantage of it as a way to intimidate those around him.

"Report," he ordered.

"Mission completed," Agent Seven replied.

Tain did not show his relief. It would not do for his agents to know their true worth. "When?"

Seven gave him the stardate. "46722.4."

Two evenings ago. "Where are you now?"

"I have just departed the planet Balancar in my own shuttlecraft."

Tain sat back. "Well done. Report to base camp Alpha-5 for debriefing and surgical alteration."

Seven nodded, unsmiling, even though agents considered it a reward to be sent to Alpha-5. It was the most luxurious base camp maintained by the Obsidian Order.

Tain waited to be sure she didn't offer additional information. Agents who had made mistakes during their mission often showed uneasiness at this point, dreading to report complications.

"Any problems?" he finally asked.

"None that I am aware of." Her eyes gazed evenly at him, like clear blue glass.

That's why Tain liked Seven. She was an empty vessel, waiting to be filled by his orders.

"Proceed to Alpha-5," Tain told her, before signing off.

If only everyone were as useful as Agent Seven. If only Gul Dukat had some weakness, then Tain would not have so much trouble with Central Command, the military arm of the Detapa Council. Gul Dukat followed in the footsteps of his father, who had opposed Tain's goals and methods. That's why Tain had ordered his own son, Elim Garak, to covertly plant evidence against Dukat's father. That evidence had resulted in his execution.

Sadly, Tain realized that Garak had never pleased him as Agent Seven did. Garak had barely managed to complete the mission to implicate Dukat's father. Then Tain had arranged to send him to distant posts to keep him away from Gul Dukat. Two years ago, when Dukat had been forced to step down as Intendant of Bajor, Tain had sent Garak to Terok Nor. Now Garak served as security chief to Kira Nerys. Meanwhile, Gul Dukat had gained a great deal of power in Central Command, and he relentlessly continued to investigate the circumstances of his father's arrest.

Tain checked their current location and found the *Groumall* was just entering Klingon territory. Once again, Agent Seven had impeccable timing.

Tain had stayed in self-imposed isolation on board Dukat's starship, so the Cardassian crew members were startled as he strode through the corridors. He didn't bother moving aside, but forced the others to step out of his way. Even if they didn't know his face, they recognized the Obsidian Order emblem on his chest. Tain didn't need to be surrounded by guards or aides for protection. The reputation of the Obsidian Order did that for him.

Tain would have preferred to remain in his quarters, but he intended to hear firsthand what the Klingons said about Duras's death. By the time Tain reached the bridge, the *Groumall* had already been stopped by a Klingon patrol.

As Tain stepped off the turbolift, Gul Dukat was saying, "I look forward to celebrating the spirit of your fallen warrior."

A female Klingon face filled the screen. "Duras did not die with honor! He was slaughtered in his bed like a feeble *targ,* his neck snapped by the hands of a woman."

Tain silently moved forward to see Dukat's reaction.

The gul grew very still, his intelligent eyes resting thoughtfully on the irate patrol captain.

"Who did it?" Dukat demanded.

"The *chab* is being hunted down now." The Klingon growled as if menacing the killer herself.

Tain found the exchange quite enlightening. The Klingon captain would be willing to talk to Cardassians only if they weren't suspects. So Agent Seven's cover was holding, and his plan to set the Klingons at each other's throats was working perfectly. That's why he had recommended to the Detapa Council, the ruling body of the Cardassian government, that they agree to hold the Alliance gathering on Khitomer.

Dukat appeared to reach the same conclusion as the patrol captain, considering this an internal Klingon affair. The gul calmly made the required arrangements for the *Groumall* to follow the patrol through Klingon territory to Khitomer.

Yet after the Klingon captain signed off, Dukat sat frowning in his chair. He did not acknowledge Tain's presence on the bridge, but surely he hadn't missed his entrance. No one turned his back on the head of the intelligence service.

Gul Dukat was different, though. As a renowned military leader in Central Command, he made it a practice to ignore Tain's importance and that of the Obsidian Order in the Cardassian Union. That was all right; Tain actually preferred it when Dukat didn't focus on him.

So Tain was intrigued to see the gul struggling to hide something from his bridge crew. His usual smug smile had been displaced by irritation.

Finally Gul Dukat gestured Tain over to the command chair.

Adjusting his uniform, Tain joined Dukat. His own expression was bitter, even suspicious. It wouldn't do to let Dukat know how much interesting information he was revealing.

Dukat's voice was low, but he demanded sharply, "Did you have anything to do with this?"

Tain smoothly retorted, "I find your interest in this death curious. What is the Duras family to you?"

Dukat glanced around the bridge, obviously trying to contain his anger. "Nothing, as you well know."

"Duras proposed a trade management plan for the Alliance territories." Tain watched him closely. "Now if it is approved, he will not be able to assume the post of Overseer."

Dukat muttered, almost to himself, "I would rather win it honorably than by default."

"You intend to claim the post?" Tain probed.

Gul Dukat did not answer, but he had already said enough.

Tain suddenly realized he had been manipulated. The Detapa Council had agreed in its last closed session that it was best *not* to create an Overseer's post. So Tain had sent Agent Seven to assassinate Duras as the cleanest route to destroying the plan and creating internal Klingon strife. Then Worf would no longer claim a majority on the Klingon High Council, and his control of the regency would be shaken. The Cardassians could replace Worf with their own Regent to be in charge of the fallen Terran Empire.

But Dukat clearly believed that not only would there be an Overseer's post, but that Central Command would back him for the position. Dukat might be self-righteous, but he wouldn't presume to overstep his bounds with his fellow military leaders. He must have assurances, even guarantees, perhaps from the Detapa Council itself. Natima Lang, head of the Detapa Council, was also on board the *Groumall,* but Tain had not spoken to her since the Detapa briefing that had resulted in his order to assassinate Duras.

It was absurd. Dukat was a military man, not a trade administrator. Tain knew that any one of the half-dozen candidates he had recommended to the Detapa Council were better suited to assume the post of Overseer, *if* the post was created. Some were deep undercover Obsidian Order agents.

Before Gul Dukat could order him from the bridge, Tain said, "I will be in my quarters. Inform me when we reach Khitomer."

Tain left the bridge without waiting for Dukat's answer. He didn't like being duped by the Detapa Council, and he didn't intend to let them get away with it. He had plenty of favors he could call in, plenty of informants to let him know who had masterminded this plan to make Dukat a power in the Alliance.

As Tain returned to his quarters, he considered the consequences. If Gul Dukat gained the position of Overseer of the Alliance, he would be influential enough to access the closed records of his father's trial. He might have the leverage he needed to discover Garak's involvement in the evidence. As Overseer, Dukat could recall Garak from Terok Nor and interrogate him. Tain had no doubt that Garak would crack under torture once his cranial implant had been removed. Garak would denounce Enabran Tain for masterminding the plot to plant incriminating evidence against Dukat's father. Dukat could make it a crusade to destroy everything Tain had worked for, perhaps even forcing him to retire from the Obsidian Order.

No, he could not allow Gul Dukat to gain the post of Overseer. If Tain hadn't realized that the Detapa Council intended to place Dukat in that position, it might have succeeded. Tain shuddered at the idea that Dukat had come so close to gaining his most cherished desire—repudiating his father's guilt.

Tain knew it was time to deal with Gul Dukat, once and for all.

Among Tain's equipment was a miniature particle ejector with cylinders of microscopic nanites. He programmed one cylinder containing ten thousand nanites as passive recording devices. Later he could remote-trigger them and retrieve up to an entire day's worth of conversations, with the nanites working together for redundancy. They were capable of recording through tissue from inside the lungs or intestines. Some would even cling to the target's hair or clothes for a day or so.

It was a technology developed by the Obsidian Order's research and development team. Tain had not shared the existence of this technology with anyone else in the Cardassian empire.

When the nanites were programmed, he loaded them into the ejector. It was a simple matter to implant the particle ejector in his lip. He could trigger the release with a certain pressure, then blow the nanites toward their victim.

At some opportune point, he would get close to Gul Dukat to murmur a few words of warning about Regent Worf or the Duras family. It would be enough. With one exhale, the nanites would disperse through Dukat's body, and then his every word, his every plan, would be available to Tain. He would finally find the lever that he needed to destroy Gul Dukat.

Chapter 4

THE KLINGONS MISCALCULATED, Deanna Troi thought to herself. They had carved this great round chamber deep beneath the surface of Khitomer in the iron-rich orange-and-rust bedrock. The walls were lurid in the yellow lamps, and the rough texture reflected the Klingon aesthetic. The Cardassians would have polished everything to a high luster, giving the eye nothing to rest on as the walls curved into the ceiling.

Troi certainly felt safe so far underground, knowing that a Romulan attack could not penetrate to this level. They would have to crack Khitomer in half to reach the twelve delegations that had gathered from across the Alliance.

Yet the Klingons had miscalculated in the design, slotting each of the twelve delegations into one-twelfth of the circle. By facing them off, territorial boundaries were emphasized, which did not bode well for a cooperative exchange.

It was the little details that people didn't notice on a conscious level that often determined the outcome. As Troi could have predicted, everyone in the hall was acting as if they had to fiercely protect their territory. Why didn't people consult her on things like this? After all, she was an empath and understood better than anyone the need for the proper psychological environment to be established.

She would be sure to mention it to Worf—much later, long after the meetings were over. Worf had already complained last night about the structure of the hall. He was forced to stand in the middle of the room with eyes boring down on him from every direction. She wondered if Gowron had deliberately placed the Regent in the center of the chamber to weaken him. That would be a subtlety she hadn't expected from Gowron, and it deserved further investigation. Gowron appeared to be responsible for a great many things lately, including Duras's death.

Since Duras had been killed, the Klingon delegation now consisted of High Chancellor K'mpec, Councillor Gowron, and Martok, the one-eyed general who commanded the empire's defense forces.

"*SoQ!*" Worf roared out, silencing the cross talk among the delegations. "*I* am Regent! You will speak to *me.*"

Bravo, Troi thought to herself. Worf needed to regain control of this meeting. She had earned a seat at the gathering because of her position as Intendant of Betazed, though everyone was well aware that her home system offered nothing substantial to the Alliance.

Troi's power was built on her close relationship with Worf.

But in reality, the two delegations who had the final decision were the Cardassians and the Klingons, the original Alliance members who had fought and conquered the Terran Empire. The outlying empires of the Breen, Ktarians, Ferengi, and Tholians had a certain autonomy since they had never been subdued by the ancient Terran Empire. They had joined the Alliance in their efforts on the Romulan front.

Of the Intendants who were present, three had been appointed by the Alliance to control once-vast empires that had been subdued by the Terrans: Bajor, Orion, and Trill. A few of the other Intendants controlled key systems such as Sol, Andor, or, as in Troi's case, Betazed. Not present were the hundreds of Intendants of the other systems and colony planets that had been subjugated first by the Terran Empire and then by the Alliance. They would have to accept whatever the key members of the Alliance decreed.

As the delegations ceased their rumbling, the Cardassians activated the light on their board, requesting permission to speak.

Troi could tell that Worf would rather ignore the request, but the Klingons could not afford to alienate the Cardassian delegation. Because of her intimate bond with Worf, she felt his agitation as he granted leave for Natima Lang, head of the Cardassian Detapa Council, to speak.

Lang was accompanied by two male Cardassians. Gul Dukat was a renowned military leader, and Enabran Tain was head of the Obsidian Order. Troi had interacted with Dukat at former Alliance gatherings, especially when he had served as the Intendant of Bajor for several years. Dukat had always been a forceful, honorable man . . . for a Cardassian. But she had never seen Enabran Tain before, and his presence at this gathering emphasized the importance of the debate.

"We've talked for two days, and we've read the reports." Lang glanced at the other delegations, then turned to look pointedly at the Klingons placed directly across from her. Another error, in Troi's opinion. "The lack of coordination in trade matters is clearly having an adverse effect on our profits and production levels. We have enough information to decide whether an Overseer post should be established."

Without waiting to be recognized, the Andorian Intendant called out, "You are delaying the vote, Klingon!"

Worf bellowed a challenge and leaped over the railing encircling the central dais. With two strides, he reached the Andorian table and grabbed the Intendant by the front of his leather vest. The Andorian's antennae bobbed as he tried to jerk away. Worf bared his teeth into the vivid blue face, which was now looking distinctly frightened.

"You forget your place," Worf said harshly. "You are here because *we* allow it."

With his feet lifted off the floor, the Andorian Intendant sank into his vest, his hands scrabbling against Worf's armor. Only his white hair and curving blue antennae could be seen.

Troi gasped as her body reacted to Worf's surge of energy. She felt his exhilaration as the Andorian struggled helplessly in his grasp. Yet she could also sense the Andorian's emotional reaction, his rush of adrenaline as he was brought eye-to-eye with uncontrolled ferocity.

Troi had seen Worf kill with less provocation. For a moment she thought the Andorian was going to die. The Andorian himself thought he was going to die. Everything slowed to this one moment, as if her own body hung suspended over the void by a fragile thread, every nerve zinging, every muscle clenched, every sense fully alive . . . The distant voices of the other Alliance delegates cried out, echoing against the rough stone walls . . .

But this time Worf did not kill. Worf thrust the Andorian Intendant away, and he fell back among the half-dozen members of his delegation, who tried to support him.

Worf turned away with a growl as the rest of the chamber was silenced. Trembling with desire, Troi met his eyes. They exchanged a private look, knowing they would take these feelings into their private chambers tonight. Then the clamoring delegations demanded Worf's attention.

Troi hardly listened, savoring the unexpected gift of pure sensation. She lived for moments like these, unlike most Betazoids who shunned the rest of the galaxy, preferring to remain on their slowly recovering planet. Three generations after the Terrans had been defeated, their garden world was finally beginning to bloom again after the ravages that had been inflicted on it.

After the Alliance had won, Betazoids had gone into

self-imposed isolation. The empaths and telepaths were convinced that their continued safety relied on total seclusion. Especially after the Klingon and Cardassian armada destroyed the Lethean race. The Letheans had successfully resisted Terran control by using their telepathic ability as a weapon, delivering a severe, usually fatal telepathic shock to their targets. The Alliance had feared the Letheans as much as the Terrans did, and had utterly decimated the alien species.

Troi knew that many Alliance officials were wary of her power to read emotions, and it gave her a negotiating edge that she usually tried to conceal. From time to time, in the decade she had been Intendant and lived by Worf's side on his flagship, some Betazoids on her home planet had proposed complete withdrawal from the Alliance. But calmer heads had cautioned that they should maintain vigilant eyes on the quadrant.

Or at least, that's what Lwaxana, her mother, reported in her weekly communiqués. Lwaxana was the daughter of the Fifth House, Holder of the Sacred Chalice of Rixx, Heir to the Holy Rings of Betazed. Since Troi preferred to live off-world, she had been named Intendant, though her influence over the ruling houses of Betazed was minimal.

So Troi dutifully reported back every week on the state of affairs in the Alliance, and received a chatty letter in return about the weather and the petty antics of the Betazoids in her mother's social circle. Troi knew she would have died of boredom by now if she had stayed on Betazed.

Meanwhile Worf's irritation was increasing as the arguments continued over the need for a trade Overseer. Troi released the tension on her mental blocks, necessary in such crowded conditions, and happily readied herself for another explosion of raw emotion.

Then Kira Nerys, Intendant of Bajor, requested permission to speak. There was no one else at her table, in marked contrast to the crowded Breen and Ktarian sections. There were also numerous Andorians who were now scowling at the other delegates for not protesting the shocking way their Intendant had been treated by the Regent.

"I, for one, would like to commend the Regent," Kira stated firmly. Her red hair and wrinkled nose looked playful, while her tight black skinsuit shimmered seductively whenever she moved. "I've heard no complaints about the military leadership of the Alliance territories, so there is no need to undermine the Regent's authority." Here Kira paused to smile graciously at Worf. Troi narrowed her eyes at Worf's grunt of approval.

"I think," Kira continued, "the Overseer *must* report directly to the Regent. After all, the Regent has the final word on any action that would support the Overseer's needs. The Overseer would merely serve as the focal point of communications, to better facilitate the trade needs of Alliance members with the hundreds of colonies and planets in the former Terran Empire."

"Better," Worf stated flatly.

"Of course," Kira agreed, "this is closer in spirit to your original proposal, and it would solve the problems we've seen in the reports. I suggest we break to let our tempers cool, then reconvene to decide whether this would be acceptable."

Troi was intrigued when Worf agreed, obviously not realizing that Kira had taken control of the meeting. Several other key delegations—Breen, Tholian, and Orion—also signaled via a flashing red light their agreement to Kira's proposal to break.

Worf temporarily halted the proceedings.

Thoughtfully, Troi observed as the delegations stood and moved about. Kira immediately began speaking to the Breen High Administrator. Troi had not expected much from the Bajoran Intendant, who had only served for two standard years. Yet Kira Nerys had been instrumental in forcing the Alliance to remove Gul Dukat as Intendant over Bajor, reminding everyone that it was supposed to be an interim appointment after Intendant Opaka had been killed. Troi had watched with interest when Kira had been challenged for the Intendant's post by Winn Adami, the First Minister of Bajor, who subsequently lost her appeal to the Alliance. After Kira had become Intendant, Troi had considered the wily Bajoran worthy of careful observation.

"Do you require anything, m'lady?" Keiko asked softly.

Troi smiled at the Terran serving girl. Keiko was a recent acquisition, an exotic beauty who was unassuming and pliable. B'Elanna, the Sol Intendant, had given Keiko to Troi on their last visit to the Utopia Planitia shipyards.

"Yes," Troi told Keiko. "Go fetch the Grand Nagus of Ferenginar. I wish to speak with him now."

"Yes, m'lady," Keiko said, bowing her head.

While Keiko ran her errand, Troi carefully entered the

outer ring that surrounded the delegation tables. Doors opened off this ring, leading to private waiting chambers for each delegation.

Troi timed her exit perfectly to meet Gowron, who had just left the Klingon table, two delegations from hers. Gowron was startled by her sudden appearance, and he regarded her with distrust. Most Klingons accepted her simply because she was the Regent's companion, but Gowron had never trusted her because of her empathic ability.

"Do the Klingons still support their original Overseer proposal?" Troi asked Gowron.

"I never supported that proposal," Gowron snapped. His bulging eyes shifted nervously.

"But you will take the position if it is offered to you," Troi told him, knowing he couldn't deny it. She fully opened her empathic senses to absorb every nuance of Gowron's reaction. "The death of Duras has changed many things."

His face darkened and he hissed, "*You* are not to speak of that!" His finger was suddenly close to her face, pointing at her to silence her protest.

Troi wasn't sure which ritual or custom she had just violated. Most Klingons lived in a terribly rigid society. Worf was more lenient about Klingon tradition because he understood that personal honor was paramount.

Yet her question had given her what she sought. It was clear that Gowron felt no guilt over Duras's death. He was not trying to conceal anything from her.

Suddenly she was sure that Gowron had not killed Duras. It was not what she had expected. This morning, she had insisted that it must have been Gowron. Now she would have to tell Worf to look elsewhere for the killer.

Troi returned to the Betazed table, allowing her Terran serving boy to settle her robes around the tall-backed chair. She waved the boy back as Keiko returned, bringing the Ferengi Intendant.

Zek hobbled forward with the help of the Grand Nagus staff. Like all Ferengi, Zek's enormous ears and knobby bald head were his dominant features. His skin was rubbery with age, and his lobes distended nearly to his shoulders. He was so old that wrinkles formed even in the sagging wattle beneath his chin. Troi couldn't bear to look at the profusion of gray hair bristling from his ear holes.

"What a pleasure, my dear," Zek wheedled in his high, nasal voice. "We so rarely get to speak anymore—"

"We met a fortnight ago on Callonda IV," Troi interrupted. She didn't like dealing with Ferengi because their four-lobed brain made it impossible for her to read their emotions. Zek seemed pleased at having an immunity to her powers.

"You said you would give me your answer on those gaming licenses," Troi reminded him.

"Ah, yes, so I did." The Grand Nagus tottered over to the chair brought by Keiko at Troi's gesture. "My memory is not what it used to be!"

"Perhaps it's time for a new Ferengi Intendant to be appointed." Troi flicked a piece of beetlesnuff from her robe as Zek sniffed up a generous pile from his gnarled fingernail.

"Not likely!" Zek sang out, laughing off her insinuation. "Appointed for life, my dear. We Ferengi know how to strike a bargain, and who better than the Grand Nagus, eh?"

Troi's lip curled as he chortled and rocked, sniffing up more snuff. She couldn't touch him, and he knew it. But she could touch his profits . . .

"I have waited long enough," she told Zek. "Decide now. If you don't agree, I'll transfer all trade in the Betazed sector to the Trill. They are eager to franchise establishments in my sector."

Zek's smile faded. "But we're in the middle of negotiations . . . and the Overseer will have the last word in trade agreements."

"If Kira's suggestion is agreed upon," Troi countered with a bland smile, "the Regent will remain in control of the Overseer."

"Yes . . . that is her plan," Zek agreed. "She has some interesting ideas about trade. But why not put a Ferengi in charge of trade, eh?" Zek leaned forward, his tone growing conspiratorial. "I'll give you those gaming licenses for Betazed and the surrounding sectors if you support my candidacy for Overseer."

"What?" Troi drew back in disgust. "The Alliance would never agree to give you the post. You would manipulate it to suit your own needs."

"And you're any different?" Zek shot back, his nasal tone gone hard. "Don't *you* count on getting the job, dearie. If anyone is less likely to be Overseer than me, it's you."

Troi stared at him, knowing that he was merely stating the truth. But she hated the way it sounded. She shuddered at the sight of his jutting, pointed teeth, stained with snuff slime. Disgusting.

"Decide now." Troi raised her hand slightly. "And remember the one hundred ninety-second Rule of Acquisition: 'Never cheat a Klingon unless you're sure you can get away with it.'"

"Ahh," Zek murmured, glancing at the Regent, who was shouting at one of the members of the Tholian delegation. "There is that . . ."

"Then you agree? I receive a fifteen percent agent's commission and control over the gaming licenses in the specified sectors."

"Fifteen percent on the net profits," Zek bargained.

Troi had expected that all along. "Agreed." She gestured to Keiko, who smoothly produced a padd for the Grand Nagus.

Zek read it over, hemming and hawing, but Troi refused to negotiate further. She merely pointed out that the meeting was about to recommence, and the Grand Nagus finally pressed his thumb into the padd.

"It's a pleasure doing business," Troi lied. She got none of her usual satisfaction in feeling her victim squirm.

But with this deal she would control the gaming licenses in nearly a dozen sectors surrounding Betazed. She could close down the competition and force everyone to come to the new resort she intended to build on Betazed II. Her people had barely begun to colonize the extra Class-M planet in their system . . . and Troi knew that a luxury resort on one of the remote island continents would be a perfect place for her to live. She was tired of the nomadic life on Worf's flagship. She intended to create her own galactic salon, where the best and most prestigious people would come for the finest entertainment and luxury in the galaxy. In order to make it appealing, it would also have to be the premier gaming establishment in that region. Her lifelong dream was finally coming true.

She hardly paid attention as the Grand Nagus left her table. She signaled the padd to report the transaction to the computer of the *Negh'Var,* where it would be logged in the Alliance records. Then she slipped the precious padd into an interior pocket, knowing she wore a private, satisfied smile.

When the conference recommenced, only Troi dissented when the twelve delegations voted to support Kira's proposal to appoint an Overseer under the Regent's jurisdiction. The others agreed that the star systems of the fallen Terran Empire needed to be better managed and coordinated with the independent Alliance empires. Basically, the Overseer would be in charge of the Intendants of each sector. It would be a powerful position, which was why Troi voted against it.

Now the jockeying began for a candidate to become Overseer. But Troi was busy thinking about her new gaming licenses. The Ferengi may be loathsome, but their Rules of Acquisition were an inspiration. During Worf's angry outbursts about the gathering, she had kept in mind the 162nd Rule: "Even in the worst of times, someone turns a profit."

Every delegation except hers proposed candidates for the Overseer's position. Troi would not subject herself to public discussion in this manner, and she kept out of the fray. But Grand Nagus Zek threw in his name, as did the self-righteous Andorian Intendant. Some of the more interesting candidates were Gul Dukat, the Orion Intendant, and Kira Nerys.

Troi sat back to enjoy the battle, for it was sure to be a good one. She didn't care who won. Her goal for this gathering had been accomplished.

Chapter 5

KIRA NERYS WAS luxuriating in a Nelavian milk bath when Gul Dukat was announced. She kept the gul waiting in the reception room on her private starcruiser, *Siren's Song,* while she completed negotiations with the Orion Intendant. Varinna was a tempting green humanoid with dark hair and startling red lips. She was also the head of the Orion Syndicate, and ruled the vast Orion Empire with a firm hand. Yet she was in the same position as Kira, pressured by the increasing material demands of the Cardassians and Klingons.

"Then we have an agreement?" Kira shifted slightly to see the Orion. Varinna was languidly rising from the low chaise where she had eaten choice delicacies from the hand of a Terran slave. Soft string music made a pleasant complement to the rosy glow in the room. In the center was a sunken mosaic-tile pool, surrounded with silk and satin brocade sofas. The long gilded mirror on the ceiling reflected Kira in the pool, her red hair nicely complemented by the minty green Nelavian milk. The room was a miniature replica of her pool chamber on Terok Nor, and it was her favorite room on the newly built *Siren's Song*.

"I agree to your proposal." Varinna settled her gauzy skirt as she stood next to the pool. "You will give the syndicate the concessions we discussed in exchange for the Orion vote for you as Overseer. But secrecy is key."

Kira laughed. "Then you better give Gul Dukat a reason you're here."

"Bring him in," Varinna ordered the slave.

Kira was amused and gestured for Marani to obey. As the door opened to let Gul Dukat enter, Varinna bent and gave Kira a thorough kiss. Her voice was low, "That should confuse matters nicely."

"It's my pleasure," Kira responded warmly.

Gul Dukat hesitated in the doorway, as if he had barely caught the interaction and wasn't quite sure of what he had seen. On her way out, Varinna bowed her head in greeting, a sinuous gesture of graceful hands and supple spine. "Gul Dukat, fancy meeting you here."

"And you, Intendant," Dukat responded, always quick on his feet.

"I was just leaving." Varinna gave Kira a wave of her fingertips.

Kira pursed her lips to blow Varinna a kiss. She was delighted with the Intendant of Orion and intended to make further acquaintance with her.

Kira turned to Gul Dukat. "And what can I do for you?"

Gul Dukat stood at the end of the sunken pool, glancing around at the gold and rose furniture. Bowls of sweets and fruit stood on the tables, ready to be offered by the kneeling slaves.

His expression was doubtful. "You met with the Orion Intendant while you were in that?" he asked.

Kira lifted one arm, letting the light shine on the pale green milk that coated her skin. "I thought everyone liked green women. Varinna certainly does."

Dukat hesitated, becoming exasperated. "I can't talk to you when you're lying there."

She sank lower, leaning her head against the cushion. "Isn't this a social call? If you want to do business with me, you should make an appointment."

"Shouldn't you be completing your proposal for the Overseer's position?" Dukat countered.

"Oh, I have experts handling that." Kira smiled up at him. "That's why I would be perfect for the position. I let qualified people do the work."

Dukat's neck ridges tensed as one fist clasped the other. "You can't seriously believe *you* will be made Overseer."

"Actually, I think Varinna has a good chance of becoming Overseer." Kira laughed low.

Gul Dukat finally sat down on one of the sofas, his solid bulk dwarfing the delicate piece. "I came to speak to you about something important. I wish you would listen."

"Oh? Well, in that case . . ." Kira gestured to her slaves. They immediately leaped up and brought over a silk robe to drape around her. She strolled into the sonic shower, knowing that the frosted glass doors would reveal a silhouette of her body as the jets removed the milk.

"Would you like something to drink?" she called, smoothing her hands over her waist and hips.

"No." Dukat wasn't even looking in her direction.

Kira was pleased at being able to discomfort Dukat. She had served as his chief of security on Terok Nor for several years while he was the interim Intendant. The Intendant selection process had dragged on, giving her time to cull favor among the Alliance delegations. Kira Nerys had used the powerful Bajoran presence on the Romulan front to convince the Alliance that a Bajoran Intendant would do a better job than a Cardassian. Finally, it had seemed natural to name Kira Intendant rather than Winn Adami. The Bajoran First Minister was popular with her own people, but completely unknown outside the sector.

Gul Dukat had wanted to keep the Intendant post, and he had resented Kira's claim that he was mismanaging the Bajoran territory. He had leaned heavily on Bajor during his tenure, and insisted that the current quotas remain high for quality ore and Bajoran volunteers being sent to the Romulan front. They had been barely cordial since she had become Intendant.

So while Kira pretended to be nonchalant, she knew she must be having an impact on the Alliance gathering or she would not be able to command the attention of Gul Dukat. Suddenly, it appeared that she had a real chance of becoming Overseer.

Yesterday the discussions over who should be made Overseer had almost come to blows between the cool-headed Breen and the Andorians. That's when she had suggested they recess to allow each candidate to create a proposal for the duties of the Overseer, along with their qualifications for the job. They had two days to regroup.

Kira let her slaves wrap her in a white robe, this one edged with pure latinum embroidery. She noticed that Gul Dukat glanced at her bare feet as she approached. "If Gowron is made Overseer," she said, sitting on the sofa, "would the Cardassians really pull out of the Alliance?"

"I think the Klingons understand their request is unreasonable," Dukat said. "The Alliance is too strong to be destroyed by something like this."

"Enabran Tain seems concerned." Kira had noticed the quiet arguments among the Cardassian delegation.

Dukat waved off the suggestion. "Tain and I don't agree on many things."

Kira stored that useful bit of information, covering her interest by saying, "I suppose you know best."

Dukat missed the sarcasm. "I've been involved in Alliance politics for longer than you've been alive, Nerys. It's no wonder I understand the process."

Kira waved a slave girl forward. Marani knelt before Dukat and presented a silver dish mounded with small fruit. "Figs?" Kira sweetly asked.

"No." Dukat motioned for the slave to retreat, but she stayed in the same position, waiting for Kira's signal. "I would like to speak with you alone, Kira."

"We're alone . . . Oh, you mean my slaves." Kira gave her best patronizing smile. "Marani, take the boys and wait outside."

The kneeling slave girl, wearing little more than a scarf twisted around her body, gracefully rose and ushered the young men out of the pool chamber.

"I expected more from you than this," Dukat told Kira, gesturing to the soft room.

"You always did." Kira reclined on her sofa, tucking one leg under the other. She had hated the military discipline that he imposed on everything at Terok Nor, including the way he made her stand at attention as she gave her reports. Now it pleased her to be able to irritate him.

"I'm concerned about you," Dukat told her patiently. "I've taken a fatherly interest in your career for the sake of your dear mother—"

"Don't!" Kira sat up, holding her hand out to stop him. She had a flash of her mother's face, looking adoringly at Dukat. "Don't you talk about my mother."

"Nerys," Dukat chided. "Meru was very dear to me."

"She was your mistress." Now Kira was angry. There was no need for Dukat to bring up her mother, his mistress while he had been Intendant of Bajor. Kira had objected fiercely to their alliance, though her father was dead and her mother was a lonely woman. The affair had caused a permanent estrangement between mother and daughter. The only good thing was that no one else knew about it. As head of security on the station, Kira had been as careful to conceal it as Dukat. She had arranged secretly adjoining quarters, and had made sure she joined them whenever they were seen together in public to prevent rumors of a romantic alliance between her mother and Dukat. She had feared her mother's situation would undermine her position on the station. "She was no better than your slave!"

Dukat looked genuinely upset. "I made Meru very

happy until her untimely death. You know I tried to give her everything she wanted."

Kira stood up, tightening the robe around her. "If you came to talk about my mother, then I'm not interested."

"No, Nerys, sit down." Dukat tried to smile as he urged her to stay. "I was trying to compliment you on the job you've done as Intendant of Bajor. I always wanted the best for you—"

"You tried to keep me from becoming Intendant!"

"I didn't think you were ready. But I'm trying to tell you now . . ." He made an aggravated sound. "Nerys, would you please sit down?"

Kira slowly settled on the cushion, realizing Dukat was getting to the real reason he had come.

Dukat's hands spread wide. "I wanted to tell you that I was wrong." He lowered his head, grimacing slightly at the effort it took to admit it. "I will do what I can to help you and Bajor. I can arrange to have the quotas eased on the uridium ore shipments and the conscripts for the Romulan front . . ."

"What makes you think that's necessary?" Kira demanded.

"I commissioned the projections of the mining operations, Nerys. At the current rate of extraction, the Bajoran sector will be tapped out in eight standard years."

Kira knew he was right. The rapid depletion of Bajor's natural resources was a constant source of anxiety for her. Dukat and the Intendants before him had stripped the system of its uridium, buying Bajor a seat at the Alliance table.

"Let me guess," Kira said. "All I have to do is vote for you for Overseer."

"You know I have a special fondness for Bajor and I understand the needs of your territory." He leaned forward, his eyes lit up. "We can work together again, for the good of Bajor and the Alliance."

"And Cardassia," she said quietly.

"Yes, for the entire Alliance. It is the reasonable thing to do. A Klingon Regent and a Cardassian Overseer. The power would be balanced."

"So it appears." Kira glanced down, picking at the latinum edging on her robe.

"Then can I count on your vote?" Dukat asked.

"How can I say no?" she countered, smiling at him.

Dukat beamed, taking her question for an agreement. "Then you will not submit a proposal. Already the Trill and the Breen have withdrawn their candidates."

"If the field narrows too much, it could alert the Klingons," Kira told him. "I'll stay in a bit longer, just to confuse the issue."

"Very well, but withdraw before the vote. I want to send a clear signal to those who are wavering." Dukat rose, indicating their interview was over.

"Of course you do," Kira murmured noncommittally. She remained seated on the sofa.

Dukat paused before opening the door, sniffing the air. "Bajoran lilac. That was your mother's favorite, too."

Kira's fingers twisted in the robe, ripping the latinum threads through the more delicate silk. But she didn't let her anger show on her face. She merely nodded and smiled as Dukat let himself out.

When her slaves peeked in to see if she needed them, she waved them away. Gathering the robe around herself, she paced back and forth, giving vent to her fury at Dukat's arrogance. Who did he think he was? Coming to her ship and ordering her around as though she still worked for him.

Kira hadn't been serious when she proposed herself as Overseer, never believing she would be able to acquire the position. Yet she had received unexpected backing from the Orions. And while the Trill and the Breen appeared to lean toward the Cardassians, they had made overtures to negotiate with her. Much to her surprise, many of the delegations believed it would be disastrous to have a Cardassian Overseer and a Klingon Regent. They feared the other empires would be squeezed to death between the superpowers. Yet having both the Regent and Overseer loyal to the Klingons was not acceptable either.

Surely Dukat would not have suffered through their interview if he didn't think Kira was a likely candidate. But he had made a mistake reminding her of her mother, Meru. Kira had chafed under Dukat's rule, unsure which she hated more—his officious, condescending attitude toward her or the smarmy way he had coddled her mother in her presence. She even hated the secrecy that she had insisted on.

No matter what she said to Dukat, she would not vote for him as Overseer. Somehow, she would have to make sure she got the post herself.

Kira impatiently rang the bell. "Hurry, get me dressed," she ordered her slaves.

She might as well go to the Klingons first. In particular, she would start with Regent Worf. Why begin at the bottom when she could find out right away whether she had a chance of success? She could probably swing the Breen and Trill toward her if she had the Regent's support.

Humming as she was dressed by her slaves in her distinctive black skinsuit, she knew that one way or another, she would beat Gul Dukat.

Chapter 6

THE FLICKERING TORCHES cast uncertain shadows as Worf and B'Elanna warily circled each other. The footing was uneven, in the best tradition of Klingon sparring grounds. Onlookers were gathering around the outer edge of the Khitomer courtyard.

The blades of their weapons shone briefly whenever they caught the torchlight in the mist. The flames made a hissing sound from the moisture in the air, like a constant hovering menace.

B'Elanna was using her *mek'leth,* a large curved saber with three points. The handguard had a lethal edge and served as a smaller blade to deflect the swings of Worf's *bat'leth.* The *bat'leth* had greater reach, as did Worf, but the *mek'leth* was a more versatile weapon.

B'Elanna fought with every bit of strength and speed she possessed, refusing to restrain herself in the face of the Regent's assault. *"QI'yaH!"* she grunted, letting his blade slip along hers as she spun away. The tip of her *mek'leth* caught his upper shoulder, slicing through the leather jerkin and leaving a gaping hole over his chest.

"*QaD!*" Worf roared. Few people got past the Regent's guard.

Worf's face was contorted with fury as he battered B'Elanna back with his *bat'leth*. She couldn't sustain her attack in the face of his superior strength, and the convex cobblestones made her less agile than usual. When she tried the *Mow'ga* feint to slip away, Worf hooked her handguard blade with a backward jab.

Her feet slipped out from under her, and she landed on her back. Her *mek'leth* was held ready, but she was looking up the curving silver point of Worf's *bat'leth*.

Baring her teeth, B'Elanna refused to yield.

Worf's eyes widened. "*Jegh!*" he ordered.

"I won't surrender!" B'Elanna declared.

"You *will* yield." Worf pressed the point against the base of her throat.

She could feel the sharp edge cutting into her skin. But she spat in defiance, "*Qo'!*"

B'Elanna was pinned to the stones, and as her refusal echoed through the hush, she realized that no one on the sparring field moved. The eyes of the Khitomer locals were riveted on the Regent's match, waiting for what he would do next.

Her heart was racing as she looked up at him, but Worf's eyes crinkled, the first sign of his pleasure.

"More *burgh* than ten warriors!" He laughed in approval, removing the blade from her throat.

Sitting up, B'Elanna rubbed her neck, then looked at the blood on her glove. "Thanks . . . I think."

The other Klingons were nodding and commenting loudly on the match. B'Elanna flushed, but it was a good sign. Whispering would be an insult.

Worf reached down. "It had to be done."

B'Elanna grabbed hold of his gloved hand and let him pull her up. "I know." Grimacing, she wiped her neck again, smearing the blood down her bared chest in the armor. Let them all see! They had questioned her strength long enough.

Worf clapped her on the shoulder. "Good match." Quietly, he added, "They see you are not so *Terran* after all."

B'Elanna grunted, glaring at the other warriors as she and Worf left the sparring field. The burly men and women moved aside courteously. She was short compared to them, and her build was slender. But now they knew that Klingon steel ran through her.

Worf led her into the resting chamber he had requisitioned for the duration of their stay on Khitomer. He was sparring almost every day to vent his frustration at directing the Alliance gathering. Worf's aide, Grelda, was just finishing the daily sensor sweep, ensuring that the chamber was sealed against eavesdroppers.

"Ale," Worf ordered. Grelda pulled off his gloves, folding them on the table before leaving to fetch the Klingon ale.

B'Elanna waited for Worf to give her permission to sit before settling on the stone bench opposite him. The Regent's temper was renowned, and he could turn on his favorites instantly if he thought they were being disrespectful.

Taking a sip of the ale that Grelda brought for them, B'Elanna considered her unusual relationship with Worf. Like Worf, she had grown up in the Duras entourage. B'Elanna's mother's family had served the Duras family for generations, so not long after B'Elanna could hold a knife, she had been sent from the Alliance trade vessel her mother commanded to live with the Duras family, then called the House of Ja'rod. B'Elanna had acted as an aide even though she was the same age as B'Etor. She had left the household only to serve on posts that Duras had arranged. It didn't matter that B'Elanna knew nothing of her father's family or that he had been Terran. Duras had claimed her.

It was Duras who had proposed B'Elanna as the Sol Intendant when it became clear that the system was being mismanaged. A significant Free-Terran population of mechanics, engineers, and scientists lived in Sol, and they resisted the tactics of the former Klingon Intendant. It had been a compromise to appoint a half-Terran as Intendant. High Chancellor K'mpec had protested and nearly carried the High Council, but Duras had made a rousing speech on behalf of B'Elanna. He insisted that the Klingons must maintain their hold on Sol at all costs. Since no other candidate was as uniquely qualified, B'Elanna was given the post.

B'Elanna had done well, working with the Free-Terrans and easing some of the harsh restrictions on their lives. The Terran and Vulcan slaves were better managed as well. It was not as difficult as B'Elanna had feared. She discovered that some Free-Terrans had welcomed having Earth razed to the ground by the Alliance rather than see the harsh Terran Empire continue to subjugate other worlds. Though Sol was one of the poorest systems and among the most devastated by the fighting, the colonies on Mars, Jupiter, Saturn, and Europa still had some of the busiest ports in the Alpha Quadrant because of the intersection of ancient trade lines around Earth. The Alliance also relied on the vast shipyards of Utopia Planitia to produce vessels for their armada.

With the support of Duras and Worf, B'Elanna was the first Intendant to properly manage the Sol system since the Alliance had conquered it. Her position was growing increasingly secure with each passing year as she gained the respect of the High Council and the rest of the Alliance.

Her eyes went to the shield of the Duras family, displayed in a place of honor among the weapons on the wall. She would have been nothing without Duras, nothing but a casual byproduct of her mother's vagabond life.

Worf raised his glass. "Duras will be avenged!" Taking a huge swallow, he rinsed his mouth and spat the rest on the stone floor.

"I would like to claim that honor." B'Elanna also drank. Bloodwine was the only thing fit for such a toast.

"That honor will be mine," Worf vowed.

She slammed down the goblet and stood up, pacing back and forth in frustration. "*Hegh* to Gowron's family!"

But Worf didn't say a word, though he was usually quick to curse Gowron. She had lived by her wits for too long to ignore his reaction. "What is it?"

Susan Wright

Worf shook his head, silently drinking. The slashed tunic was a reminder that she had almost bested him.

She faced him, her hands on her hips. "Why don't you challenge Gowron before the High Council?"

His fist hit the tabletop. "I do not believe it was Gowron." His voice lowered reluctantly. "Deanna says he is not involved."

B'Elanna shook her head. "Is she sure?"

"There is other evidence."

She slowly sat down at the table across from him, leaning forward. "Tell me. What do you know?"

He considered her for a moment, but B'Elanna held his gaze. "My crew have analyzed the blood found in the flyer. The woman was not Klingon. She was genetically altered to pass a routine scan. The sensors on the flight padd also detected the residue of an energy signature."

"It must have been a hired assassin," B'Elanna guessed. "With a bio implant."

Worf grunted. "The question is, who sent her?"

B'Elanna clenched her fists so hard she shook. "It's not an honorable way to kill."

Worf flatly agreed, "Not worthy of a Klingon."

B'Elanna chewed her lip briefly. Suddenly things were not so simple. "Have you told K'mpec?"

"Soon," Worf told her.

"Could it be the Cardassians?" she asked.

"The scans reveal nothing conclusive. Yet I am loath to appoint a Cardassian as Overseer."

"Not if there's any chance they killed Duras!" B'Elanna exclaimed. "I would swear blood oath this moment—"

"You must not speak of this," Worf ordered.

"But why?"

His leather jerkin creaked as he leaned back. "The Romulan front is held by Cardassian troops along the central axis. If the Alliance is shattered and military units pull out, Romulan troops will pour into the Alpha Quadrant near Klingon territory."

"But Duras must be avenged! Or he'll never reach *Sto-Vo-Kor.*"

"You leave that to me," Worf said bluntly. "We shall strike to the very heart of Romulus. In our mighty battle, Duras will gain his rightful place in *Sto-Vo-Kor.*"

B'Elanna realized she would have no say in the matter despite her relationship with the house of Duras. Swallowing her resentment, she tried to be satisfied that their enemies were in sight and they would pay for their transgressions.

But there was one thing she did want. "Request permission to continue the investigation of Duras's death. The Sol scientists can be quite adept at deciphering sensor readings."

"Granted," Worf agreed readily. "I will have the logs sent to the *Sitio.*" The *Sitio* was her flagship, aptly named "military siege" in an ancient Terran language.

"I'm glad it wasn't Gowron's doing," B'Elanna admitted. "We don't need a Klingon civil war right now."

Worf agreed, "We shall face the Alliance delegations as a united front."

Though their anger simmered under the surface, both were able to sit and drink their ale, letting the sweat cool from their bodies. There were few people B'Elanna felt as comfortable with as Worf. Duras had been her closest ally, and Worf had become a true friend. Worf had arranged the sparring match to impress the gathered Klingons. Her defiance of the Regent would be talked over tonight in every alehouse on Khitomer.

Grelda entered the chamber, bowing before Worf. "Regent," she said, "the Bajoran Intendant is here, requesting permission to speak to you."

"Kira Nerys?" Worf asked. B'Elanna was surprised. The Bajorans were usually allied with the Cardassians and had nothing to do with Klingons.

"Yes, sir. She's here with several attendants."

"Show her in." Worf gestured to B'Elanna. "Wait behind that door. She will speak more freely if she thinks we are alone."

B'Elanna took her ale and went into the bathing room. By leaving the door open a crack, she could hear as Kira Nerys was shown into the Regent's rest chamber. The Bajoran woman was concealed beneath a red cloak and mask, obviously donned to avoid unwanted attention as she was processed through the spaceport and carried down the streets of Khitomer. The attendants were similarly cloaked.

B'Elanna shifted for a better view through the narrow crack as the slaves removed Kira's cloak. There were two young men and a graceful, mature woman, clearly of Terran descent. Kira posed briefly to let Worf get the full impact of her skin-tight, shimmering outfit.

"Regent Worf," Kira started in an ingratiating tone. "It's so *kind* of you to see me on such short notice."

Worf grunted noncommittally as Kira seated herself

on the very bench B'Elanna had just vacated. B'Elanna wondered if the stone was still slick from her sweat.

Grelda moved forward to ask if Kira would like anything. "Klingon ale," Kira replied without looking at her. When Grelda returned with the goblet, the female slave took it and sipped before handing it to Kira. B'Elanna wondered if Kira lost many slaves that way.

Worf was offended. "Only Cardassians poison ale!"

"Cardassians have long arms," Kira replied smoothly. "I could be an accidental victim."

B'Elanna wondered if the Bajoran knew something about the assassination of Duras. Worf also leaned forward, his interest piqued. "Is this about the Cardassians?"

"In a manner of speaking." Kira smiled, tucking her chin in to look at Worf from the tops of her eyes. "I think there are matters in which we have common interest."

Worf silently dismissed Grelda. B'Elanna understood why. He wouldn't speak in front of so many witnesses.

Kira caught his glance at her slaves. "I would send them away, but it's dangerous for Terrans to be among Klingons. Could you let your woman watch over them?"

Worf nodded shortly. "They can wait in the anteroom."

Kira caught the female slave's hand, stroking it while watching Worf. "They are my pets, and I probably dote on them too fondly."

B'Elanna was sickened without realizing why. Then she thought of her mother. She had never bothered to ask if her father was a Free-Terran or a slave her mother had kept for amusement. She didn't want to know the truth.

Worf clearly wasn't impressed. When the slaves had

left and they were finally alone, he demanded, "Speak your mind."

"My, you *are* direct." Kira seemed amused. "It's about the Overseer's position."

"It is said Bajor supports Gul Dukat."

"Really?" When Worf remained silent, Kira marveled, "Isn't it amazing what people will say?"

B'Elanna wished she could burst out of hiding and kick that smug look off Kira's face. Why couldn't she simply say what she meant?

"I think there's a better option," Kira told Worf. "One that will give us *both* what we want."

"*I* want Gowron to be Overseer," Worf retorted.

"Come now, Regent, we both know you don't really mean that. Besides, none of the Alliance delegations will agree. Except for maybe the Cardassians. After all, then they could use it as justification to replace *you*. Can't have too many Klingons in the top positions, now can we . . . ?"

B'Elanna drew in her breath. She hadn't thought of that possibility.

Worf was rubbing his hand over his mouth. Clearly it was something he had considered. Still, he insisted, "I will not work with a Cardassian Overseer."

Kira drew back slightly at his vehemence. "There is another way, one that preserves your power."

Worf relaxed slightly. "How?"

"I've always appreciated your vote for me as Intendant of Bajor. That's why I suggested that the Overseer should report to you."

Worf didn't reply. B'Elanna knew he had supported Kira's claim merely to remove a Cardassian from the post.

"Since the Overseer reports to you," Kira continued, "what if *you* vouch for a candidate? You could speak privately to each of the Intendants before the vote. It would establish a precedent that the Regent selects the Overseer."

"My candidate would have to win the vote," Worf pointed out.

"Yes, it must be a candidate who already has the confidence of a sizable number of delegations."

"Who is that?" Worf asked.

Kira ducked her head in false modesty. "Me."

"You?" Worf put back his head and laughed in disbelief. "You are the newest Intendant. Who would vote for you?"

"The Breen, the Trill, and the Orions. And Bajor, of course."

That caught Worf off guard. He stared at Kira for a moment. "Can this be true?"

"I've broken their confidence, but for the price of gaining the Regent's support, I think it's worth it. And I would always have your needs in mind while doing my job . . ."

Very smooth, B'Elanna thought. Not that she believed Kira would think of anyone's needs but her own. Yet she sounded as if she was telling the truth when she said those other delegations would vote for her.

Kira moved closer to Worf. "It would solve all of your problems."

Worf seemed interested in the proposal. At the very least, he was no longer dismissing it. Everyone knew Gowron didn't have a hope in *Gre'thor* of getting the post. And they certainly didn't want the Cardassians to get it.

"I will consider it," Worf told Kira. He stood up to clasp forearms with her.

Kira leaned in. B'Elanna had to strain to hear her whisper, "I will be *very* grateful, Worf."

Not if Deanna Troi finds out you're trying to seduce the Regent, B'Elanna thought. She shuddered at the idea of what Deanna would do if she knew.

Kira laughed and lightly touched Worf's bared chest through the slashed jerkin. His skin was shiny dark with sweat. "Tell B'Elanna to vote for me, too. Everyone knows she does what you say."

B'Elanna bit her tongue to keep from protesting out loud.

"As for Deanna Troi . . ." Kira continued, "it's clear she makes up her own mind."

Kira laughed, obviously remembering the public fight between Worf and Troi during Kira's battle to become Intendant of Bajor. Worf had voted for Kira while Troi supported Winn Adami. B'Elanna had never known why Troi distrusted Kira—until now.

Impatiently, B'Elanna waited while the slaves were called back in and Kira was swathed in her vibrant cloak and mask. When Grelda finally followed them out of the chamber, B'Elanna burst from behind the door. "You can't trust that woman!"

Worf waved her off. "I trust no Bajoran. But she makes good points."

"I wouldn't count on anything she says," B'Elanna said gloomily.

"It will set precedent." Worf mused over the word, as

if that appealed to him. "The power to appoint the Overseer, with a token approval by the Alliance. That is . . . appealing."

"As long as it's the only thing that's appealing."

Worf glanced at her, as if unsure of her meaning. Clearly he was caught up in his own vision of what this would bring. "She meant nothing by her remark."

B'Elanna wasn't sure if he meant Kira's belittling comment about her. It stung because there was some truth to it. B'Elanna would do whatever Worf asked. With Duras now dead, her loyalty had shifted to Worf where it rightfully belonged. But that didn't make her a lap-*targ*. She was acting honorably, as a Klingon should.

Chapter 7

ENABRAN TAIN OPENED the secured channel at the pre-arranged time. While his personal encryption node completed the task, Tain performed a level-5 scan of his living quarters on board the *Groumall*, Gul Dukat's *Galor*-class starship. It was unlikely that Dukat could counteract his advanced methods of blocking surveillance, but Tain took great care in sweeping his quarters several times a day. He would be glad when the Alliance gathering was over so he could return to his protected bunker deep inside Cardassia Prime.

When Tain opened the encrypted channel, the face of a slender Cardassian male appeared on the screen. He wore a plain uniform that identified him as a health care professional. *"Menocc here, Ser,"* he said crisply.

"Report," Tain ordered.

"Of the four agents in residence, three have been released to active duty. However, Agent Seven of Corps

Nine is suffering physical complications and will require an additional period for recovery."

"Elaborate."

"Agent Seven was prepped as a Klingon for her last assignment as per your orders. She then used the mobile surgical unit to transition to Trill, then Klingon, then Andorian within the space of a few days. This has caused a rejection of the primary grafts. Since she did not allow herself to heal, the DNA loops were unable to seal on the genetic resequencing, which has damaged the attach nodes." Menocc keyed his unit, and the image of a Terran female appeared on the screen. *"I have returned Agent Seven to her original genetic template and physical appearance for the recovery period. The severe reddening and swelling indicates subdermal nerve damage that requires regeneration eight times every solar cycle."*

Tain examined Seven's face. It was unfamiliar to him. When Seven first came to the training facility, she had appeared to be a normal Cardassian girl who eventually matured into a plain yet majestic woman. Now her skin was puffy and blotched with red patches. Her lips were full and she had a slightly cleft chin—like a pale infant's face. He was unsure whether Terrans would consider her attractive. All Terrans looked alike to him.

"Why have you made her hair that color?" he asked in revulsion. Yellow hair was not common among Cardassians.

"That is its natural state," Menocc replied, his tone indicating agreement with Tain.

The image turned slightly, revealing more of her shoulder-length yellow hair, swept back from her forehead. Her nose and cheekbones were the most prominent features of her face. There was an EM-bandage curving over one eye and another on her temple. One hand was encased in an EM-glove.

"That's enough!" Tain ordered.

The image disappeared and Menocc was back on screen. *"The agent's fingers suffered damage during the mission, triggering the interrogation unit in her cranial implant. I have reset the implant, and I recommend an extended period of leave to complete the medical repairs."*

"Granted." After one look, Tain didn't question the seriousness of her condition. "What is her psychological state?"

"Agent Seven destroyed the mirror in her room, but otherwise she is adjusting well to the treatment. She has partaken in the pleasures offered to her, and states she is eager to return to the field."

"Do what you think is best," Tain told Menocc. "Once she is sufficiently recovered, release her to limited duty."

"Understood, Ser," Menocc said, bowing his head slightly.

Tain cleared the channel, content to put the matter out of his mind. Agent Seven would soon recover and would continue to serve him well. It was unfortunate, however, that he had been deceived about the aim of the Detapa Council. If he had known the assassination of Duras would benefit Gul Dukat, he would have ordered Agent Seven to botch the assignment.

The Alliance gathering would reconvene in several hours, but Tain still didn't have the information he needed to control Dukat. He had periodically down-

loaded the nanite receptors implanted in Dukat, but no
useful conversations had been recorded during the opening days of the conference.

Gul Dukat left the *Groumall* yesterday and hadn't returned since. Tain couldn't download the receptors unless Dukat was in close proximity. Since the receptors
were almost tapped out, Tain was uncertain whether he
would get additional information from them.

He was not beaten yet, but Natima Lang had informed him last night that Dukat had gathered commit-
ments from seven delegates for their votes. There was
little time left for action.

Tain signaled the transporter room, "I will beam
down to the starport. Prepare an escort team."

Deep inside the bedrock of Khitomer, Tain settled behind the table provided for the Cardassian delegation.
From his observation of his fellow delegates, Tain believed he was the only one comfortable spending so
many consecutive days under tons of rock. Although the
hall was crude, it reminded him of his command bunker.
He remembered how his family used to complain about
always staying underground. They simply could not understand that frequent trips to the surface compromised
the security of the Obsidian Order.

Tain was the first to arrive, but soon a few more delegates and their assistants appeared in the round hall. His
attempt to analyze their covert and overt interactions resulted in some interesting, obscure connections. The
Breen and Trill seemed to have a common interest. Natima Lang had claimed they both supported Dukat, but

they did not treat Tain in the same manner. It was revealing the way they turned away from each other as if subconsciously comfortable, yet the Trill Intendant stiffened when Tain nodded slightly at her.

Intriguing. But useless without additional information.

When Gul Dukat finally arrived, the hall was filling rapidly. Tain remained at the outer table, knowing that Dukat would retreat to the Cardassian waiting chamber to get away from him. Each delegation had their own waiting chamber adjoining the ring behind the tables. Tain would have to download the receptors inside the waiting chamber; doing so in the hall would set off the surveillance alarms.

Tain waited until Dukat was settled inside the waiting chamber before following him in. His tricorder was in his large pocket, and he operated it with one hand while nodding to the assorted aides and requesting a glass of cold fish juice. Dukat reclined in a comfortable chair, grinning as he spoke low to Natima Lang. He was looking overly confident, and he disdained to acknowledge Tain's presence.

From long practice, Tain barely felt his own reaction of annoyance. Personal feelings tended to interfere with executing the job. Staying near the door, Tain tapped out the retrieval sequence. The vibration of the unit indicated the receptors had been downloaded.

Tain accepted the frosty glass of fish juice and returned to the outer table.

Quickly, he downloaded the receptors into a searchable database. He keyed in a command to find any conversations between Dukat and the other delegates. Five appeared altogether. The Breen conversation was approximately two minutes long, cut short by the senior delegate after a cursory agreement to support Dukat's candidacy for Overseer. Tain was not convinced; he was reminded of that old saying, "Never turn your back on a Breen."

Dukat's next conversation was with Kira Nerys, the Intendant of Bajor. Tain noted Dukat's irritation when she received him in her bath. Even more important was the presence of Varinna, the Orion Intendant, when Dukat arrived. He heard nothing to explain why Varinna was meeting privately with Kira.

Tain skimmed the transcript, noting Kira's strong reaction when Dukat mentioned her mother. He had been aware that Dukat had kept Bajoran mistresses while serving in various posts. It was unusual, but as long as Dukat's indiscretions had occurred outside Cardassian territory, his superiors would not deign to notice them.

As for the Overseer's post, Tain was not impressed by the way Dukat so blatantly tried to flatter and bribe Kira. The Bajoran Intendant did not actually agree to support his candidacy for Overseer. Instead, she had asked, *"How can I say no?"*

Perhaps Dukat's bid for Overseer was not as firm as he believed.

There was something else in their conversation . . . Tain scrolled back up and reread the lines spoken by Dukat: *"I am concerned about you. I've taken a fatherly interest in your career for the sake of your dear mother—"*

That gave Tain an idea, a way he might be able to gain

control over Dukat. Most of the women who had been Dukat's companions were no longer alive, which was suspicious in itself. But what if one of those unions had resulted in offspring? A half-Bajoran child could be devastating to Dukat's career if it was brought to Cardassia Prime. Tain's own cultural aversion to mixed-race individuals made his lip curl in disgust. Other species may not mind mixing alien bloods—just look at that half-Klingon, half-Terran Intendant of Sol!—but Cardassians knew better. Such mixtures were an abomination.

Tain marked the conversation and made a note to authorize a thorough investigation of Dukat's alien mistresses. Feeling much better, he continued skimming through the transcripts recorded by the nanites. Nothing quite as interesting turned up, but Tain gathered that Dukat had never actually spoken to the Orion Intendant. He had made arrangements with an aide, who agreed the Syndicate intended to support him.

Just before the conference recommenced, Kira sauntered around the outer circle, speaking briefly to someone in every delegation. Tain watched her approach, alerted by her glance in his direction. The Bajoran woman moved sinuously, seemingly drawing the delegates closer with each word. The clinging black jumpsuit accented her hips and chest, typical humanoid erogenous zones. Tain was one of the few who could see through the beguiling affectations. He knew that Kira proceeded around the room with a great deal of determination.

"Sitting out here all alone?" Kira asked him, pausing

next to the entrance to the Cardassian table. She ignored the closed door behind her that led to the waiting chamber.

Tain lifted the tricorder with a polite smile. "Some reading to catch up on."

"I'm glad I have this chance to speak to you." Kira smiled in a particularly intimate way. "I was chatting with Gul Dukat yesterday, and he said that you two don't always agree. I thought that was interesting, seeing as how *I* don't always agree with Gul Dukat."

"Is that so?" Tain asked rhetorically.

"But of course, you know that. Dukat didn't want me to have his post as Intendant of Bajor. I believe I won that time."

"Indeed you did," Tain agreed, considering her carefully. Her light manner hid a deeper purpose, which she did not intend to reveal now.

"Perhaps we can work together to our mutual benefit in the near future." Kira smiled and nodded, moving on to the Ktarian delegation.

Intriguing . . . Tain made a note to add Kira Nerys to his priority list.

The delegates took their seats at the tables, and the conference recommenced. Worf called for candidate proposals. B'Elanna, the Orion Varinna, the Breen, the Trill, and the Ktarian Intendant had all withdrawn their proposals, leaving six candidates: Gul Dukat, Gowron, and Kira, along with the Andorian Intendant, the Tholian Emperor, and the Ferengi Grand Nagus.

Dukat flushed when Kira submitted her proposal,

glaring in the direction of the Bajoran delegate. There was a visible strain puffing up his neck ridges. Natima Lang gave Dukat a brief, quelling look. Tain remembered how Kira had evaded Dukat's question about withdrawing her candidacy before the vote.

Worf called a break so the delegates could have two hours to consider each proposal. Tain spent the time thoroughly analyzing the transcripts of Dukat's conversations picked up by the nanite receptors. The telemetry report indicated that he wouldn't receive any more information from the empty nanites.

But they had served their purpose. Tain began outlining the search parameters on Dukat's former mistresses and assigned the job to two of his best research agents.

In his tricorder, Tain tagged the issue as priority one: a project that required daily updates. Soon he would find the information he needed to destroy Gul Dukat.

After everyone had reviewed the candidates' proposals, the first vote was to narrow the field to three candidates. Dukat, Gowron, and Kira tied with three votes each. The other three each received one vote and gracefully withdrew, except for the Grand Nagus, who demanded a recount. His request was bluntly denied by Worf.

Now Gul Dukat was visibly angry at Kira. There was a long debate over the relative merits of the three candidates, and it became clear that some delegations feared the destruction of the Alliance if a Klingon or a Cardassian became Overseer.

There was further debate about the advisability of a secret ballot for the final vote. The Alliance had always conducted business openly to make sure each delegation was responsible for its vote.

During the argument over the sequence of voting, Dukat retreated to the waiting chamber to calm down, on the advice of Natima Lang. His irritation was not serving him well, with the delegations coolly examining his reaction. Tain was inwardly pleased, realizing that Dukat had not judged the situation correctly. Now he couldn't quite face reality. Tain had never seen Dukat so vulnerable.

While Dukat was gone, Tain took the opportunity to say to Natima Lang, "Dukat is taking this too personally. It could force the swing votes toward the Klingons."

"That would be disastrous," Lang murmured, her outward demeanor reserved.

"I would prefer that the Bajoran take the post rather than the Klingon. She has worked well with us in the past."

Natima glanced at Kira, who was conducting herself correctly. The Bajoran Intendant noticed both the Cardassians watching her, and she raised her glass slightly in respect before sipping the beverage it contained.

"Dukat believes she betrayed him," Natima said quietly.

"Dukat may be mistaken," Tain countered bluntly. "He is a military man, not a negotiator. He was mistaken about the Breen and the Orions. The Breen have sided with the Trill and are supporting the Bajoran Intendant. I believe the Orions will now vote for Kira, as well. That is four votes."

Lang examined the delegations. "I should have put myself forth as a candidate instead of Gul Dukat. But since he had been an Intendant, I thought that he would be considered more qualified."

Tain realized what she was saying. Lang was all but admitting that she had chosen Dukat as the Cardassian candidate for Overseer. Despite years of undercover duty, Tain almost couldn't hide his reaction. So that was why Dukat was overconfident. He knew he had Lang's full support. Or rather, he used to have her support, until he had started acting like a petulant child being denied a toy.

"You could have won," Tain quietly agreed.

After that, he let the matter drop. He pulled out his tricorder and logged in another priority-one issue—Natima Lang. Lang had never openly defied him, but she had rarely cooperated with him, either. Now Lang had deceived him into authorizing his agent to kill Duras, whose death would benefit Dukat. Tain decided that rather than endure her leadership of the Detapa Council any longer, he would prefer to deal with any one of the legates who would take Lang's place. He had in mind certain events he could set in motion that would ultimately result in her being ejected from the Detapa Council.

However, everything depended on this vote.

Tain balanced his tricorder on his leg, tapping in notes and comments about the various members of the delegations. He paused to look around carefully. This was one of those occasions when tensions ran so high that people inadvertently revealed themselves.

Lots were drawn to determine the order in which the delegations would vote. The Cardassians were first, while the Intendant of Sol and the Klingons were last.

The first four delegations—Cardassian, Andorian,

Ferengi, and Tholian—voted in favor of Gul Dukat. Then there were four votes for Kira from the Breen, Trill, Orions, and Bajorans. Dukat hissed under his breath when Varinna cast the Syndicate vote against him.

The Ktarians were next, a delegation that most present had not paid much attention to. The tiny Intendant stood at his table, the horns on his forehead going white with tension. "We vote for Gul Dukat!"

Dukat was beaming as if he had personally created the little man. "That's five," Natima murmured. "We shall have it!"

Tain realized that she could be correct. If the Klingon, Sol, and Betazoid delegations voted for Gowron—as everyone expected—then Dukat would lead with five, while Kira had four. There was great consternation at the Klingon table as this fact became clear.

Indeed, as Deanna Troi, Intendant of Betazed, stood and cast her vote for Gowron, the tension rose. Then the Intendant of Sol got to her feet. "Sol votes for . . . Kira Nerys."

The half-Klingon's expression was sour, and it was clear she felt she had no choice. Lang's gasp indicated her concern. Dukat sat forward, his smile abruptly gone.

K'mpec heaved himself to his feet, his leather creaking in the suddenly silent chamber. "The Klingons choose Kira Nerys!"

In the uproar that followed, Tain noticed that Kira saluted Worf. Apparently they had created this arrangement in order to keep the Cardassians out of the Overseer's post.

Dukat was livid. "She's only been an Intendant for two years!" he shouted to the gathering.

"Better she than you!" K'mpec retorted, standing up.

The Andorian Intendant shook his fist at Worf. "This was your doing!"

"I demand a recount!" Zek called out in his penetrating nasal voice.

The Breen were already packing up to leave, as were the Tholians. Apparently the gathering was breaking up in a shambles, but the Alliance appeared to be intact. Kira gracefully withdrew to her waiting chamber, and her slaves guarded the door. Already she was running from the condemnation of her fellow Intendants. B'Elanna of Sol looked as if she wanted to hit someone hard, while the Andorian Intendant continued to yell at Worf until the burly Klingon made a menacing move toward the blue man.

Tain laughed out loud, his first real enjoyment of this sort of meeting in decades. It had been worth every hour he had spent outside his bunker. Dukat was not the Overseer, but neither was a Klingon. Now he would have time to consolidate his position and get some leverage to use against both Gul Dukat and Natima Lang.

This Bajoran, Kira Nerys, was turning out to be very interesting. Perhaps, as she had suggested, they could work together sometime.

Still laughing quietly so as not to openly antagonize Dukat, Tain retreated to the waiting chamber. It would be good to get back to his command bunker on Cardassia Prime.

Chapter 8

BENJAMIN SISKO SLUNG the carryall over his shoulder as he left the airlock of his patrol cruiser, *Denorios,* named after the Denorios Belt in the Bajor system. Captain Sisko had just completed the long trip to the Alliance outpost near the Romulan front. The outpost was a patched and repatched conglomeration of an old Cardassian station joined to a series of Tholian drydocks. The welding seams bulged where the docks met the station, with the faceted Tholian structural beams uneasily abutting the gray curving plasteel typical of Cardassian architecture. The outpost was suspended alone in space, ready to retreat under impulse power at any adverse turn in the fighting on the front.

Sisko wore a Trill pilot's helmet and flight jumper, knowing that his dark skin would help hide the lack of spots. Terrans were usually slaves, and though Sisko was among the 2 percent of Free-Terrans, he didn't like to take chances. Most Cardassians or Tholians would have no compunction about "acquiring" a new slave, so he took precautions against discovery. His crew had their own best interests at heart in concealing the secret of his identity. When he was in the Bajoran sector, it didn't matter. He always had Kira Nerys for a backup. What a woman! She would fight the Detapa Council itself to get him back.

He was probably thinking about Nerys because the outpost reminded him of Terok Nor, his home base. But these corridors were narrower, and he had to duck to get through some of the adjoining hatchways. Despite the similarities, Sisko did not feel comfortable here, and it wasn't only the ominous proximity of the Romulan front a few light-years away. He was uneasy about the presence of Alliance officials representing the empires who were united against the Romulans. These bureaucrats tended to get in one another's business, squabbling over amenities. He had to be careful not to step on anyone's toes.

But that wouldn't stop the other seven crew members of the *Denorios* from enjoying the pleasures offered on the war-torn station. Rather than joining them, Sisko had two meetings to keep. His official duty of conveying the monthly cargo of duotronic chips was already completed, the manifests having been checked and certified by the docking master.

Now it was time for his real work to begin. He made his way through the teeming life-forms that filled the Promenade, heading directly for the lockers at the rear. Sliding the carryall into a cubicle, he sealed the mechanism with his handprint. The carryall contained several thousand sticks of *sub rosa,* a pleasure-inducing chemical that was prized by the soldiers stationed on the ships at the front.

The Alliance didn't object to the sale of *sub rosa,* as long as it was properly taxed. But these sticks were unstamped, and if he was caught with the shipment, it would mean a stiff fine and maybe real trouble if he was discovered to be Terran.

Sisko could never resist a challenge. Now, after dozens of exchanges, the practice was almost routine.

But the trade-off would have to take place later. Now, he went to his favorite gaming court on the upper levels. It was not the best gaming court on the outpost, but he preferred its dark ambience.

On the upper level, small rag-sen tables lined one wall. Rag-sen was a more intimate game than dom-jot or dabo, which often drew a crowd of onlookers. Rag-sen was played by two people using round cards.

Sisko paused next to an occupied table and dropped a thin slip of latinum into the counter in the center. The Bajoran seated at the table looked up from his padd, then added his own slip. The light flashed on the outside of the counter, indicating that both players had anted the same amount and that the currency had been analyzed to contain the proper metal content.

Sisko slung his leg over the opposite chair. "Ready to lose, Paqu Denar?"

"I heard you were in port." Paqu waved his hand over the slot in the table, and a thick pack of round cards emerged, computer shuffled and ready to be dealt. Paqu looked down his wrinkled Bajoran nose as he quickly dealt the cards.

They played silently, for very high stakes. Sisko won most of the hands. A drawer filled with strips of latinum slid open when Paqu thumbed the sensor to indicate he had lost the game. Occasionally, Paqu would win a game to keep casual observers from noticing anything unusual. But everyone on the station was busy, frantically getting what they could before being shipped back to the front. The noise was unremitting, as if the vacuum of space itself rang from the sound.

Paqu Denar was the Bajoran Supplies Officer for the outpost, and he had made an arrangement with Kira Nerys to skim 2 percent off the top of Bajoran supply shipments. By paying off Sisko, her bagman, through a friendly game of cards, Paqu didn't risk discovery of the transfers of latinum. He could chalk it up to gambling debt.

Sisko hadn't known how to play rag-sen when Kira had explained his part in the latinum transfer. At first he found the round cards confusing, and he sometimes played any card, knowing he would win regardless. But Paqu had insisted that he do a better job or they would be discovered. The Bajoran's contempt didn't bother Sisko, but gradually he had become nearly as good as Paqu. Often he stayed to play a few low-stakes hands with other patrons.

Sisko's pouch was getting heavy when he calculated that the month's payoff was almost complete. He started to wave his hand over the slot to get a fresh pack of cards, when Paqu stopped him. "We're done for today."

Sisko frowned. "But you're short."

"A handful of strips," Paqu shrugged. "There were overruns this month that I couldn't anticipate."

"That's your problem."

"It's our problem," Paqu retorted. "And I have a way to correct it." His foot nudged something that brushed against Sisko's calf. It was a bag approximately two hands long and nearly as tall. "I recently acquired this artifact from a Breen who was convicted of treason against the Alliance. It was associated with him, so unfortunately I can't risk selling it here. But you can easily get more than five slips of latinum for it elsewhere. Preliminary analysis indicates it is tens of thousands of years old."

"Listen, I'm just a messenger. I can't take some artifact instead of hard latinum—"

"I'm going to get a drink." Paqu stood up, his voice still low. "You can sell it and get five slips or give it to your boss with my compliments. I expect you to be gone when I return."

Paqu sneered as he turned away. It was provoking, but Sisko knew that he couldn't force the Bajoran to give him the latinum. It would be up to Kira to decide what to do with him.

Sick of rag-sen, Sisko slipped the strap of the bag over his shoulder and wandered toward the dabo tables. A crowd of Bajoran and Cardassian soldiers jostled one another around the spinning wheel, but the risk was too high for Sisko to indulge. Not that he minded playing for high stakes, but there were too many people watching, captains and commanders among them. He didn't want to catch an official's curious eye.

He bullied a Ferengi out of his favorite stool in an

upper corner and watched the action for a while. Several of his crew members entered the joint, and they came up to the mezzanine to join him, bringing a rare Romulan ale for everyone to enjoy.

He considered buying a few bottles to take to Nerys. She liked little surprises. But he yawned and finally left empty-handed. It didn't pay to please the Intendant too much. He had been working for her for several years, starting when she was security chief on Terok Nor. Usually his patrol cruiser roamed through Bajoran space, exacting duties from passing ships. There were also several pickup jobs Sisko regularly performed for her. In between runs, he and his crew relaxed in favored status on Terok Nor. When the *Denorios* was in dock, he usually slept in Nerys's quarters.

It was nearly time to leave the outpost, so Sisko headed for his rendezvous with the *sub rosa* dealer. His adrenaline started pumping, as it always did during a covert deal. But the exchanges were almost boring by now. He accepted the ten strips of latinum, judging the amount by the weight of the pouch. Then he palmed opened the locker, leaving the door slightly ajar. After he left, the dealer went to the locker and took out the carryall with the *sub rosa*.

Sisko went the back way through the docking ports to reach the *Denorios*. The rest of his crew arrived while he was performing the systems check. Everything went smoothly until he received clearance. Then his second-in-command, a Bajoran named Celoni Dei, informed him that they were missing a crew member.

"It's Tidi Ilar," Celoni told him. "He may have been

forcibly conscripted. There was talk of a transport of Bajoran conscripts for the front being processed through the outpost."

The other crew members stopped what they were doing, watching Sisko's reaction. This was the danger of working near the front.

"He knows the rules," Sisko said bluntly. "If Tidi's not back by the time we get clearance, then he's no longer one of the crew."

"It's not his fault," the engineer protested. "If he was conscripted, maybe we can get him out."

Sisko shook his head. "I'm no baby-sitter. You all have a cushy job with me. If you can't stay out of trouble, I can't afford to get into it to rescue you." He sat down in the pilot's seat. "Seal the airlock."

In the back of the cruiser, someone said, "We lost Tidi . . ."

The airlock hissed, shaking the ship as it clamped shut. Sisko cleared the *Denorios* for launch.

As they passed through the security perimeter around the outpost, the patrol cruiser was abruptly seized by a tractor beam from one of the surveillance buoys. Sisko answered the hail.

A Klingon appeared on the viewscreen, his black hair standing on end and a scowl on his face. "*Denorios,* you had eight life-forms on board when you arrived, but you leave with only seven. Explain."

"This is Captain Benjamin Sisko. Perhaps *you* could explain," Sisko retorted, leaning back comfortably in his command chair. "One of our Bajoran crew members was conscripted while we were in port."

"Prepare to be boarded for inspection," the Klingon ordered.

"I don't think so," Sisko said slowly. "We're scheduled for a pickup at Terok Nor for the Intendant of Bajor. She would be very . . . irritated if we were late."

"It is against procedure to allow—"

"Well, if you can hand over my crew member now, I'll take him along. Otherwise, I have a schedule to keep." Sisko didn't have anything hidden on board, but it was a matter of principle to keep Alliance officials out of his business.

Behind the irate patrol guard, a female Klingon approached. There was a muttered exchange, but Sisko heard her say, "That one belongs to the Bajoran Intendant. Better let him go."

Sisko felt a flash of anger, but the Klingon was growling, "Begone, *Denorios!*"

The tractor beam disengaged. Sisko forced a grin, lifting one hand palm up. "See? I knew you'd be reasonable."

The Klingon broke off transmission, but Sisko felt somewhat better. Everyone was a toady, one way or another, doing what someone else ordered them to do.

"Take the helm," he told his second.

"Aye, sir." The man avoided his captain's eyes. Obviously he was wondering if Sisko would have been just as indifferent if Celoni himself had been conscripted. Sisko usually liked a touch of fear in the crew's eyes. It kept them on their toes. If none of them could afford to lose their post on the *Denorios,* that kept him safe.

But Sisko was reminded of something in Celoni's expression, a look of hurt from a betrayal. Jennifer had looked at him that way whenever he returned after disappearing for weeks or when she found contraband among his gear. He and his wife hadn't been suited to each other. Sisko had finally left the Sol system and fled to the other end of the Alpha Quadrant to get away from the disappointment in her eyes. Her resigned misery had been even worse than the angry fights they used to have. He had finally given up on the whole thing. Obviously, marriage wasn't for Ben Sisko.

He retreated to his snug cabin in the back of the *Denorios,* taking the bag with Paqu's artifact. Its weight kept surprising him. Maybe it really was worth something.

Curious, he ran his finger along the seam of the bag to open it. Inside was a burnished metal object. It was round and flat, and appeared to have been buried for a long time. He flaked off some gray sediment to get a better look at the unusual incised symbols on the surface. A slight dent at one edge operated a silent mechanism that opened the object like a clam shell.

The top half was polished inside like a mirror, faithfully reflecting his bored expression. The bottom consisted of overlapping triangular leaves of metal. It was much heavier than it looked, but basically it was just another ornamental mirror.

He rested it on the computer console in front of him. It sat solidly, and he could angle the mirror to look into it. But even if age did give it value, it was dirty, chipped, and ugly. He couldn't wait to see Kira's face when he gave it to her as part of Paqu's payment. She would not appreciate being shorted. Then again, there wasn't much she could do to punish Paqu when they were engaged in an illegal activity together. But if anyone could figure out a way, Nerys would. She was something else . . .

Slowly he realized his reflection was growing dim as the mirrored half of the artifact began to cloud, obscuring his features. As he stared into it, a new image appeared. It was the tiny figure of a woman undressing.

Sisko instantly recognized Kira Nerys from her vibrant red hair. When she turned, he could see her face, remote and dreamy as her slaves slipped a sheer sleeping gown over her shoulders. The image had the depth and clarity of a hologram, as if he was really looking at Nerys.

Sisko caught his breath. This was more than a mirror . . . He couldn't believe his eyes. Was that really Nerys? In the background were rows of candles and green velvet cushions on the bed. It was the interior of her luxurious new cruiser, the *Siren's Song*.

As he watched Nerys get into bed, Sisko instantly knew that he wouldn't give her the artifact. This was too valuable. Paqu must not have examined it closely enough or he would have seen this—

Sisko suddenly felt as if he were falling forward, and when he tried to grab onto his chair, nothing was there. The artifact dissolved in front of him, as he felt himself sucked into a vortex of motion. He screamed, but the sound was ripped away before it left his mouth. He turned and flipped, trying to grab hold of something.

Sisko landed in a sprawl on the deck. For a moment he didn't know what had happened. "What . . . what was that?" he muttered, shaking his head, trying to make the disorientation pass.

"What are you doing in my quarters!" someone demanded.

The lights went up and Sisko tried to focus as a woman came nearer. In shock, he saw her red hair and wrinkled nose. She looked more astonished than angry.

"Nerys!" Sisko exclaimed. "Is that you?"

Chapter 9

KIRA NERYS REALIZED that it was her favorite pirate and occasional bed partner, Benjamin Sisko. "What are you doing here? You're supposed to be at the Romulan front."

"I am . . ." He glanced around. "Where am I?"

Kira crossed her arms. Benjamin was always playing games with her, but right now she wasn't in the mood. After she had been confirmed as Overseer, the Alliance gathering had quickly dispersed. She was already being inundated with information and requests by the other Intendants. She had staged an early retreat, but the *Siren's Song* was still days away from Bajor.

"You better explain how you got past my guards unannounced," Kira told him.

"I . . . I don't know." Benjamin got up, still looking dazed. Usually nothing bothered him, and if it did, he never showed it.

"What are you up to?" she demanded, taking another

step closer. He towered over her. "I could have you thrown in the slave compound on Terok Nor with one word."

"Nerys, I don't know what just happened." Sisko ran his hand over his crisp black hair, still looking around as if he couldn't believe it.

"You must know something. Where's your ship?"

"The *Denorios* just passed the security perimeter around the Alliance outpost. We're . . . en route back to Terok Nor."

That was dozens of light-years away. "How did you get here?"

He took a deep breath, looking down at his hands. "I was holding this artifact. Paqu gave it to me as part of his payment. He shorted you five slips of latinum, but he gave me this . . . mirror, I thought. It was only about this big, and looked old."

His open hands indicated a circle about the size of a dinner plate. He stared down as if remembering what had happened.

"I was looking at it, then suddenly I saw you getting ready for bed. Marani tied your bow." He pointed to her throat where the sheer gown was tied. "Then it felt like I was falling . . . and I ended up here."

"Let me get this straight. Paqu gave you something that transported you *here* from the Romulan front . . . for five slips of latinum? That's absurd."

"He must not have known. I can't believe it myself—"

Kira cut him off with a curt wave of her hand as she strode to her computer. She activated the direct line to the commander of the *Siren's Song.* "Prepare to verify the location of the *Denorios*. Patch me in to the second-in-command, Celoni Dei."

While she gave her orders, Sisko stumbled over to the replicator. He ordered an Aldebaran whiskey and drank it quickly. A second one materialized as Celoni Dei appeared on the screen. The Bajoran was sitting bolt upright, clearly taken aback by the sudden summons to speak to his Intendant.

"Give me your location," Kira ordered.

Celoni read off the coordinates, which Kira's computer translated onto her desktop starchart. The *Denorios* was near the Romulan front, on a trajectory that would intercept Terok Nor in six days at current speed. Kira sent the information to the *Siren Song*'s first officer and almost instantly received confirmation that the communication origin matched those coordinates.

Kira checked, but Ben was not in the line of sight of the monitor. He didn't appear to be interested in her conversation. She wasn't ready to believe him, but he was certainly not acting like his usual cocky self.

"Where's Benjamin?" she asked.

"The captain? He's in his quarters. Shall I tell him you wish to speak with him?" Celoni seemed much more comfortable with the idea of passing Kira along to his captain.

"Do that," Kira told him.

She watched as Celoni signaled the captain, then became increasingly concerned when Sisko didn't answer. The second-in-command glanced over his shoulder and ordered one of the other officers to go get Sisko.

"I'm sorry, Intendant. There must be a problem with the comm system. He'll be here shortly."

If this was an act, Kira was impressed. She didn't think the plodding Celoni was capable of such a deception. Sisko was sitting on the bed now, downing his second Aldebaran whiskey. Sweat beaded on his forehead and was running down his neck.

"He's not there," Kira told Celoni.

The Bajoran started to protest, certain that his captain was on board. But the crew member returned, her hands held out and her eyes wide. *"He's not in his quarters."*

Celoni performed an internal scan of the *Denorios,* then looked up in shock. *"He's not on board! Where is he?"*

"None of your security systems were alerted?" Kira asked.

"No! He was on the bridge not five minutes ago!"

Kira considered it for a moment. "Return at warp eight to Terok Nor. Don't stop for anything. And don't enter Captain Sisko's quarters—that is vital. Do you understand? If anything in his quarters is disturbed, I'll know it and you'll all end up in ore reclamation."

"Understood, Intendant!" Celoni looked frightened out of his wits.

Good, thought Kira, terminating the communication. She wasn't sure what had happened, but it deserved a thorough investigation. If Benjamin was telling the truth, she would find the artifact on the *Denorios.* If he was lying, well . . . she would find out soon enough.

Smiling, she got up from the computer. Sisko was still looking frazzled and confused.

"You know, you're sort of sweet like this," she told him, walking closer. "All vulnerable . . ."

Warily, he tried to draw back from her outstretched hand. "Nerys . . ."

She stroked his hair, enjoying the way he couldn't resist her. "Shh . . . I'll be gentle this time."

Kira ordered the *Siren's Song* to proceed at top warp speed to Terok Nor. She kept Ben's presence a secret by hiding him in her quarters for several days. She liked feeding him off her own plate and making him wait inside the 'fresher while she was tended by her slaves. It wouldn't do for anyone to speculate on how he had arrived so mysteriously.

Benjamin was unusually docile despite this treatment, and she knew he would give her no trouble over the artifact. He didn't want the responsibility of such power.

Kira, on the other hand, welcomed power. Before the *Siren's Song* reached the Bajoran system, she was already flexing her muscles as Overseer. She gave numerous orders to the Intendants as she scanned the data her advisors forwarded to her. They first sifted through the vast amounts of information pouring in, but she was still getting too much incomprehensible data. She would have to redistribute the work assignments when she returned to Terok Nor, since her advisors were already busy with internal Bajoran matters. The first thing on her list was to get a few more administrators who could handle the Overseer's duties.

Meanwhile, she received Worf's communiqué containing the text of every trade agreement conducted under his regency. Kira thought their first working meeting via subspace channel went well. Worf appeared eager to relinquish the onerous administrative duties so he could deal solely with the security of the Alliance.

Kira was ready when the *Siren's Song* arrived at Terok Nor shortly before the *Denorios* was reported entering the Bajoran system. She couldn't trust her security chief, Elim Garak, to deal with Sisko's crew. The Cardassian put his own self-interest first. She would have liked to get rid of Garak, but it was impossible even now that she was Overseer. Garak knew things about her that would jeopardize her hard-won position.

So she beamed directly from the *Siren's Song* to the *Denorios* herself. When she found the round artifact inside Sisko's quarters, she knew this miraculous device was exactly what she needed to defend her power as Overseer. Without opening it, she quickly concealed it in the rough woven bag. She didn't bother to tell Celoni Dei that Sisko was fine and would return shortly. Instead, she beamed directly to her quarters on Terok Nor. Later she would release Ben from the 'fresher on the *Siren's Song,* once she was sure that he wouldn't speak about this device to anyone.

Kira locked herself inside her inner sanctum on Terok Nor and performed an analysis on the artifact. It was inert when closed and resembled nothing so much as a portal on a ship. Then she carefully opened it, covering the shiny mirrored half with a silk scarf to avoid looking into it. Benjamin had said he was teleported after thinking about her and seeing her image in the mirror.

Her computer ran a comparison of the incised lines on the outside and the configuration of interlocking triangles inside. After a prolonged delay, the results indicated a strong correlation with Iconian design.

The implications were astonishing. The Iconians were a technologically advanced civilization that was destroyed some two hundred thousand years ago. An Iconian gateway had once been discovered near the Romulan front, capable of transporting many people at once across interstellar distances. The gateway had been destroyed by the Alliance armada in order to prevent a Romulan invasion.

Kira studied the images that were made prior to the aerial bombardment of the planet that held the gateway. The ancient stone ziggurat had an internal structure of neutronium, and outwardly, there were some similarities to the small round transportal on her desk. Her computer detected a large percentage of neutronium in its casing.

The Iconians had been called Demons of Air and Darkness, and it was believed their civilization was destroyed by enemies who feared their advanced technology. If this portal was a miniature version of the large Iconian gateway, it could send someone instantaneously across many light-years. She had a weapon of almost unlimited power.

After thoroughly examining the portal, Kira called for one of her slaves. Marani immediately appeared in the inner sanctum, holding several velvet-lined boxes filled with Kira's robes. She was unpacking from the voyage to Khitomer.

Kira hesitated to use her for this experiment. Marani gave exquisite massages.

"Send in Ian," Kira ordered.

Marani inclined her head, the perfect picture of obedience. Soon Ian arrived, his cheeks slightly flushed in anticipation of his mistress's orders. The young Terran could hardly have been two decades old.

Kira locked the door behind him and made him sit at her desk. She turned the Iconian portal toward him, with the base resting flat and the shiny mirrored half standing up. When she removed the scarf, it reflected his face.

Kira quickly looked away, circling behind the portal so she could see Ian's expression. "What do you see?"

"My face," he said, puzzled.

"Think about Romulus," Kira urged.

"Romulus?" he asked, looking up at her.

"Yes, the planet where Romulans come from." Irritably, she ordered, "Don't look at me, look into the mirror. And think about Romulus."

He glanced back at the mirror, then up at her. "I've never been to Romulus. I grew up in the Dahkur camp on Bajor."

Kira sighed. "Computer, show me a city on Romulus."

On the screen appeared a beautiful panoramic view of vertical towers lit by the setting sun. The light was ruddy and the clouds were purple, edged with silver. Some of the narrow spires had outspread wings at the top, the traditional Romulan bird-of-prey design.

"Take a good look." Kira gestured to the portal. "Then look in the mirror and try to image the same scene."

Ian frowned slightly, biting his full lower lip as he looked from the computer to the mirror. He checked the image a couple of times before glancing back at the artifact. He kept having to push his curls out of his eyes in order to see.

He was starting to grow desperate at failing to understand what his mistress wanted from him, when Kira realized what she was doing wrong. "I have another idea, Ian."

She leaned over and tapped on the computer panel, "Show me the Romulan Empress."

The Romulan Empress had a haughty expression and a long nose that made her face seem elongated. Even her pointed ears were larger than normal. Her robes were silver, as flat and cold as her eyes.

"Look at this woman," Kira ordered. "And try to imagine her in the mirror."

Ian took a deep breath, looking first at the image of the Empress, then at the mirror. His attempt to concentrate was enchanting. If Kira hadn't been so busy experimenting, she would have told him to give her a kiss.

It took a few moments, with his eyes fastened on the mirrored surface. Then he whispered, "I see her . . ."

Kira leaned forward. "Good, keep looking. Imagine she's in front of you."

"I see her." He reached out his hand. "So close—"

Ian's eyes and mouth went round in surprise, and he lurched forward slightly. He glowed as a light emanated from the mirrored half of the portal.

His body seemed to freeze and shrink extremely fast, as if he were sucked through an atom. Kira felt an odd displacement. She was leaning so close to the portal that for a moment she could sense the vast layers of dimensions that squeezed her own. For a moment, she understood the very nature of dimensional space.

A popping sound snapped her back into place. The portal rocked slightly on the desk. It was closed now.

Ian was gone.

Kira thoughtfully picked up the Iconian portal. With her other hand, she tapped the computer to signal Odo, the supervisor of the Terran slaves. "I'll need another personal slave, Odo. Could you send up another one with curly hair?"

The next day, the Romulan media services described how the Royal Guards had killed a Terran who suddenly appeared at a reception for the Empress, in the heart of one of their secured cities. Kira's intelligence reports indicated that Romulan officials believed he was an Alliance spy, but the frenzied guards had destroyed him before he could be interrogated.

Kira decided to try another experiment. This time she told Marani to wait inside her inner sanctum with the door locked tightly. Then Kira took the Iconian portal with her into the 'fresher and sealed the door.

Kira's hands were shaking a little as she opened the device. But she had to be sure it would work.

Holding the clamshell portal, Kira stared into the mirror and imagined she could see Marani. She thought of Marani's almond eyes, dark brows, and perfect red bow of a mouth. Lovingly, she imagined the curve of Marani's shoulders and her creamy neck, remembering how good her hands felt, rubbing and caressing her into relaxation. Marani was probably confused right now, but she would be all right . . .

That's when she saw Marani in the mirror. The slave looked uncomfortable and alone, sitting in the inner sanctum. Kira almost laughed at the way she never took her eyes off the door to the 'fresher where her mistress was hiding.

Suddenly Kira fell forward, her hands tightening on the portal. But that didn't stop her. She felt as if she were turning inside out, dropping straight through the deck.

Kira fell and landed lightly on both feet, crouching for a moment to catch her balance. Everything whirled around her, but the portal in her hand was solid. It seemed to hang in the air, keeping her from pitching forward. Somehow it had closed.

She let go, and the artifact stayed suspended for a moment. Then it fell to the deck. It rolled a short way, then spiraled down on its edge, finally coming to rest near Marani's chair.

Marani was looking at Kira, her beautiful face distorted by shock.

Kira shook her head, trying to stop the room from reeling around her. But her dizziness quickly passed.

She picked up the portal from the deck where it had fallen. She now knew that the portal would teleport through space with her if it was held. That could be very useful for getting in and out of tough situations.

"What did you see?" Kira asked.

"You!" Marani looked over at the door to the 'fresher, still sealed shut. "How did you get here?"

"Never mind," Kira ordered. "Did you feel anything?"

"Nothing." Marani was very frightened now.

"No breeze, no disorientation?" Kira judged that Marani was about two arm-lengths away. Very close, but not as close as Kira had been when she sent Ian away. "You didn't know anything was happening?"

"No! You were just . . . *here.*"

"Good." Kira fastened her eyes on the Terran. "You are not to speak of this, you understand? If I hear any rumors among the slaves, you will be my ex-masseuse."

"I would never . . ." Marani breathed.

Kira smiled and dismissed Marani, pleased with the way her slave scurried out of the room. It reminded her to return to the *Siren's Song* soon to let Sisko out of the 'fresher.

Kira locked the Iconian portal in one of the secured vaults in the inner sanctum. Truly, it was a priceless tool. With this portal, she could go wherever she wanted, or send someone wherever she wanted them to go. With this astonishing artifact, she could truly rule as Overseer and take control of the former Terran Empire.

Chapter 10

AFTER A THOROUGH survey and expert geophysical evaluation of Betazed II, Deanna Troi was certain that the string of islands adjacent to the upper continent was the best setting for New Hope, the utopia she planned to create. Sitting on the steps of the temporary housing unit erected above the Winamay Falls, she could see the hanging gardens cascade nearly a thousand meters down the layered cliffs.

She finally felt at peace. Others would feel this way, too, when they saw these vistas of natural beauty.

Of course, a force field would have to be erected to protect the resort from unauthorized entry and to temper the violent winds that raged over the tops of the cliffs, but that was a relatively minor matter.

Troi would have been very happy were it not for the thought of Kira Nerys. That upstart Bajoran was interfering with her lucrative shipping agreement with the

Orions. The modest fees that Troi had imposed to give security priority to Orion shipments to the front had been canceled when Kira established a unified system of shipping taxes. It had eliminated a quarter of Troi's income with one blow, just when she needed the resources to begin New Hope.

Troi had already obtained the agreement of certain major Ruling Houses of Betazed, using various incentives. Her best argument was that Betazed's only protection from the Alliance was her relationship with the Regent. Otherwise Betazoids had no leverage in galactic politics. But if there were a strong community of influential people who frequented her resort on Betazed II, then they would ensure that the system was not invaded or defiled.

Troi had also given large sums of latinum to the Ruling Houses, nearly depleting her reserves. The Betazed economy had suffered from their policy of isolation, and her home planet was in desperate need of infrastructure and social service improvements. The poor in rural areas were already singing praises to her name.

Troi had enough latinum amassed to continue her New Hope project, but Kira's trade manipulations were likely to cut into the luxury detailing that was important to the success of her utopian paradise. It was irritating, and despite the beautiful setting, Troi kept returning to the question of what to do about the Overseer.

Troi, more than anyone, could sense the unbridled lust for power and sensation that drove Kira. She could sympathize with many of Kira's feelings, but unlike the Bajoran, Troi preferred methods that were subtle and elegant. Kira's blatant sexuality and unrefined responses repulsed Troi. She believed they would eventually clash, and she had been anticipating a battle ever since Kira became Intendant of Bajor. Troi had refused to vote for Kira then, as she had refused to vote for her as Overseer, despite Worf's request.

Worf hadn't been angry. She had convinced him that it was better for the proud K'mpec to bow to the inevitable and vote for Kira rather than his own favorite, Gowron. K'mpec must learn to respect both her and Worf's position in the Alliance. By voting for Gowron herself, she appeared to be supporting the Klingons, while thrusting them into the position of voting for Kira rather than letting Dukat take the Overseer's position. It had been a delicious moment, one she still savored.

Troi's serving girl, Keiko, appeared in the archway behind her. "An incoming transmission for you, m'lady."

Troi almost ignored the slave so she could continue enjoying the lavender sunset overlooking the falls. But she hadn't heard from Worf in several days, and she needed to know when he would return to fetch her. Her business on Betazed was completed. She had walked through the holographic plans for Betazed II with the senior architect and finalized the design. Construction would begin as soon as work crews and materials could be brought in. She didn't need to be present for that phase.

Troi sat down at her travel computer terminal and keyed open the transmission. Her welcoming smile was greeted by the Grand Nagus on the viewscreen.

"Surprise!" Zek exclaimed, laughing and wheezing in his nasal voice. *"You look happy to see me, my dear."*

Troi was tempted to snap, "I thought you were someone else." But that would be insulting to Worf. "You wanted to speak to me?" she asked noncommittally. Where *was* Worf?

"I had to be the first to tell you," Zek assured her. *"Our deal for the gaming licenses is off."*

"What!" Troi stood up, leaning into the monitor. "You can't do that!"

Zek held up his hands and squealed, as if afraid she would come right through the screen. *"It wasn't my fault,"* he whined. *"The Overseer canceled agency fees on gaming."*

"I don't care what she's done. You figure out a way to make it happen," Troi demanded.

Zek spread his hands wide; they were almost as wrinkled and disgusting as his ears. *"I wish I could do that. But Kira is renegotiating the gaming licenses through her office. That includes the agency fees on gaming equipment."*

"Then record our transaction. We have a deal."

"The sixteenth Rule of Acquisition," Zek reminded her. *" 'A deal is a deal ... until a better one comes along.' Kira already assigned those gaming licenses, at a much better rate for us."*

"You can't do this to me," Troi said flatly. "Unless you want every Ferengi trading vessel stopped and searched by Alliance security for the next five standard years."

Zek persisted in shaking his head. *"You'll have to take this up with the Overseer. She's the one who acquired the licenses."* Zek laughed at Troi's horrified expression. *"Ta-ta, my dear. It's been a pleasure doing business with you."*

"No—" Troi started to protest, but Zek cut the transmission.

She sent an urgent message to Worf. Then she tried to calm herself by doing a few mental exercises, honing her focus and control. She was sure Worf would make Kira do what she wanted.

When several hours had passed with no word, Troi sent another message. It was quite late now, with the three moons rising in the night sky and the *lappas* filling the air with their pleasant hum. Troi was standing in the open doorway of her temporary housing module, wondering why it was taking so long for Worf to respond. Finally her travel computer signaled that she was being hailed.

Worf's dark and familiar face filled the screen, as if he was leaning very close. "Deanna, what is wrong?"

He seemed furtive, and when she caught a glimpse beyond his unruly black hair, she realized he wasn't on the *Negh'Var*. The colors were soft and muted, heavy on the pinks and gold.

"Where are you?" she asked.

"Bajor."

"You're still on Bajor?" Troi asked, astonished. "I'm done here, and I wanted to know when you would return."

"I was delayed," Worf said shortly.

In the background was the sound of a glass breaking, followed by a peal of feminine laughter. Worf looked distinctly uncomfortable.

"Who's there?" Troi demanded.

"We are working. There are many details to settle—"

"Kira Nerys is with you now?"

116

Worf's brow darkened. "We are working."

Troi tried to restrain herself. If Worf thought she was losing control, he would no longer respect her. He prized her for always maintaining her assured style when everyone else was falling apart.

"When will you return for me?" she asked quietly.

"I leave tomorrow."

Troi forced herself to nod. "I will be ready."

Worf leaned closer. "You know I long to return to you, *Imzadi*."

Troi genuinely smiled at that. She touched his cheek on the screen, then ended the transmission.

Deeply disturbed, she sat for a long time next to her computer. She believed Worf would always love her, but she didn't trust Kira. Seduction was a dangerous game. Many people fell victim to wily predators whom they didn't like or desire.

She felt as if she were under siege. Just when it seemed that everything was arranged so nicely, with a long and stimulating future awaiting her on Betazed II. Now nothing seemed certain.

Troi waited until Worf had left Bajor and was safely away from Kira Nerys before broaching the subject of the gaming licenses. She didn't intend to give him an ultimatum or force him to choose between her and Kira. The fact that Worf had been kept on Bajor for longer than necessary, along with other small signs of his enjoyment of Kira's company, made her reluctant to create a situation in which he would begin to compare her to another woman.

So, via subspace communication, Troi began by telling him about Betazed II and how well her plans were progressing. She pointed out features of New Hope that would appeal to Worf's warrior spirit—the Klingon amenities and holoprograms designed for maximum physical output. There was even a gaming ring where contestants could pit their strength and skill against one another, including, if requested, a fight to the death.

Yet Worf had never been interested in her dreams about New Hope. He preferred to be on his flagship and always would. She was also realizing the danger in letting her lover roam free through the galaxy. Not that she minded his roving eye, as long as he returned to her.

So Troi was disturbed when Worf resisted talking about Kira and the cancellation of the gaming licenses. She tried to point out how adversely this affected the development of New Hope because she would lose control of the resort if someone else placed a tariff on the gaming profits. A 15 percent fee could wipe out her margin. And if the gaming license were removed on a whim, her ability to attract the elite to her utopia would be seriously impaired. Almost every entertainment at the resort would be affected.

"It is within the Overseer's rights," Worf doggedly insisted. Only his head and shoulders showed in the monitor. *"She controls trade, including gaming."*

"But can't Intendants have some measure of control in their own sectors?" Troi was willing to give up the surrounding systems as long as she held Betazed. It was a fair compromise, in her opinion.

"Ask Kira," Worf told her stiffly. *"I am sure she will approve the gaming on New Hope."*

But at what price? Troi wanted to demand. Worf knew that she was at the mercy of whoever held the license. Kira could levy a tariff or assign the license to someone else, who could shut down New Hope out of spite or competition.

"Kira won't give me anything. Can't you order her to give it to me?"

"Now you complain of the Overseer too!" Worf exclaimed, shifting out of view of the screen in his agitation.

"I never wanted to have an Overseer, remember?" Troi said with a defiant toss of her head. "But Duras convinced you—"

"Do not speak of Duras!" His eyes narrowed, Worf glared at Troi in a way that she had rarely seen.

Troi realized she had overstepped her bounds. Worf had not yet been able to fight a battle on behalf of Duras so his friend could claim a place in *Sto-Vo-Kor.* He could not bear to hear Duras mentioned, knowing the man was in some hellish limbo.

Perhaps she should have waited until they were together to have this conversation, so she could sense his reaction. She could imagine many of the Intendants were making similar complaints.

His sullen face reminded her not to be overeager. She was slipping because she was afraid of losing her grip on Betazed II. It was vitally important for her to have a refuge from the galaxy.

However, she could not press this with Worf. Not now, and perhaps not ever.

"Very well," she agreed, inclining her head to show she would not bother him further. She managed to speak of inconsequential things, such as when he would return and where they would go next, until Worf's tension eased. It would not do to leave him angry with her. She felt ever more keenly her tenuous position, and of course, that only made her long more for New Hope to become a reality.

"My love is with you," she assured him, before signing off. But her heart was on Betazed II, and she could not let him see that.

Worf smiled—such a rare sight—and she knew everything was fine. For now.

Troi's serving girl, Keiko, interrupted her while she was sitting at the computer, staring off into the dark, star-filled sky. "Will you have your refreshment on the terrace again, m'lady?"

"I suppose." Troi stood up, yawning. As much as she wanted to live here, she preferred to have the comforts of the galaxy at hand. Her temporary quarters on Betazed II were far too rough for her taste. Yet she was reluctant to return to Betazed, where she would have to interact with her own people, including her mother.

Troi knew there was always a place for her in the Sol system. B'Elanna would come fetch her back to Utopia Planitia until Worf's return. But Troi didn't want anyone else to know how long he had been kept from her side.

She stepped onto the terrace, into the safety of the windscreen. She was enjoying the view of the moons shining on the luminous green sea at the bottom of the cliffs, when the faint sound of a scream drifted from the nearby shelters.

"What's that?" she asked Keiko.

"Tomas is being punished, m'lady," Keiko replied.

"Ah, yes." Troi remembered that Tomas, one of her Terran slaves, had been caught trying to enter the women's quarters where Keiko herself slept. Troi had inquired into the matter and found that Tomas harassed the women when no one else was around. Keiko had admitted being afraid of him.

Troi glanced at her serving girl. "Now you won't have to worry about Tomas, Keiko."

"Yes, m'lady." Keiko was stoic, as usual, with hardly a ripple of emotional reaction as the last scream faded away.

That's why Troi liked Keiko. The slave was a perfectly still pond, letting nothing ruffle her. Troi disliked having her servant's emotions interfere with her thoughts when she wanted to be alone. But she needed someone to tend to her.

Most Terrans were animals, and Tomas was the classic example of that. No wonder the Alliance had overthrown their brutal empire, enslaving the Terrans in order to contain their uncivilized and backward nature. Troi had tried to find something worthy in the Terrans she used as slaves, but the best thing she could credit them with was the sort of dumb, servile diffidence that Keiko so finely exhibited. Animals, every one of them.

And yet . . .

Troi irritably watched the slaves as they deposited the trays of delicacies on the table. She could feel the male Terran's resentment over Tomas's punishment, and the other serving woman was so afraid that she would incur the same punishment that her hands shook as she set down the pitcher of iced *slac*.

"All of you, go!" Troi ordered.

The slaves scattered, yet Troi knew there was one Terran who would always remain—herself. For most of her life she had hidden the secret of her birth. She was the daughter of her mother's favorite Terran slave. At eighteen, Troi had left Betazed soon after she was informed who her father was. For the first time she knew why others feared telepaths, and she had fled rather than risk revealing her secret to her fellow Betazoids. She had needed time to build blocks around the knowledge in her mind.

So with Lwaxana's assistance and connections, mother and daughter served as the link between Betazed and the rest of the galaxy. Troi might pretend to be a daughter of the Fifth House, daughter of Holder of the Sacred Chalice of Rixx, and Heir to the Holy Rings of Betazed. But she was really just an animal, hardly better than her own serving girl.

Troi was trembling with fear, knowing that she held on to her powerful post only because of Worf's love for her. The fact that she was thinking about her Terran ancestry indicated how tenuous her situation was. Everything could come tumbling down at a moment's notice.

Keiko approached. "A message from the Intendant of Sol, m'lady."

Troi automatically took the padd with the communiqué disc in it prepared to play. B'Elanna was also half-Terran. Perhaps that was why Troi felt a secret affinity with her.

When she initiated the message, B'Elanna's smooth Klingon face marked her as unmistakably different whereas Troi had escaped any outward mark. Indeed, Betazoids looked so similar to Terrans that her people had used that as another excuse to remain isolated rather than be mistaken for the barbarians. What had started out as a precautionary measure in the beginning of the Alliance had hardened into ironclad tradition—a tradition Troi had not felt compelled to break until she had discovered the truth about herself.

B'Elanna was shaking her head as the message began. *"I wanted to let you know that the Ferengi reopened the gaming on Utopia Planitia and the Martian Colonies. I expect all the gaming establishments in the nearby sectors will be up and running again within a day or so. There was nothing I could do to enforce the embargo you requested. Kira has taken over most of those licenses."*

Troi's fingers tightened on the padd. Of course Kira would make her presence felt immediately.

"She's also practically shut down Jupiter Station under these new export duties," B'Elanna continued. *The other systems are complaining, too. I think if we called the gathering today, not a single Intendant would vote to have an Overseer. It was the worst thing we could have done to ourselves."* B'Elanna shrugged angrily. *"Just wanted to let you know."*

Troi popped out the disc and held it up. A dangerous thing for B'Elanna to say on record.

Obviously, no one else was going to set things straight. It was up to Troi to do something about the problem.

Chapter 11

THE PUNGENT SCENT of *bateret* leaves filled the court
yard in the sprawling government complex of th
Chamber of Ministers, the legislative body of Bajo
First Minister Winn Adami was seated in her receivin
room, a blank scroll unrolled on the desk in front of he

The Bajoran Gratitude Festival was taking place, an
Winn was supposed to write her problems on the Renewa
Scroll. Then she would lead the procession of minister
into the courtyard, where their witnesses were gathered
One by one they would place their scrolls on a burnin
brazier so their troubles would symbolically turn to ashe

If only the annual celebration could so easily banis
her troubles.

Winn paced to the window, where the blue smok
curled as it drifted up the inner walls of the comple
Chanting echoed outside as her people partook in th
ancient ceremony, practiced for nearly twenty thousar

years, some historians said. The families of the other ministers were gathering in the courtyard to witness the burning of the Renewal Scrolls, but Winn had no family. Her aunt and two cousins had died at the Romulan front before she became a Bajoran minister, and she had never found time away from governing to start her own family. But over to one side were the nine children Winn was currently fostering, watched by the child-care professionals she employed. Winn could never turn a needy child away from her home.

Her enveloping robes, embroidered with the symbols of her *D'jarra*, protected Winn from the chill air. This day officially marked the new season, heralded by the tiny stalks of *baylets* poking through the soil, yet it still felt like midwinter.

There were some who protested the symbols on her robes, preferring to forget the old days when Bajoran society was ruled by a system of castes. A family's *D'jarra* used to dictate social status as well as the occupation its members could hold. But the Terran Empire had destroyed the ancient Bajoran caste system, and the Alliance had imposed a surface equality that reconciled many to the fact that they were no longer free.

Most Bajorans would protest that they had been freed when the Terran Empire was destroyed, but Winn knew better. That was why she had covertly joined the Circle in fighting the Alliance.

"Are you ready, First Minister?"

Winn turned to see Tora Ziyal, one of her administrators, standing in the doorway. Though Ziyal was barely past her second decade, she had faithfully served Winn since being fostered in her home as a child. Ziyal's heritage was written on her face, where Cardassian eye ridges and forehead depression met a wrinkled Bajoran nose. But Ziyal had grown up on Bajor and was Bajoran to her core. Like most Bajorans, Winn was not one to discriminate. They had learned their lesson about xenophobia from the Terrans who had once enslaved them.

"Is something wrong?" Ziyal asked, approaching Winn.

Winn gestured to the empty scroll. "I cannot choose among my problems."

Ziyal smiled sympathetically. "You are not limited to one, First Minister."

Winn sighed and seated herself at the desk. "Tell the ministers I will be with them shortly."

"As you wish, First Minister." Ziyal hesitated. "You said you were not to be bothered, but the Intendant of Betazed, Deanna Troi, left a message for you to call."

Winn looked up. "The Regent's companion? For me?"

"Yes, First Minister. I thought you would want to know."

"Thank you, Ziyal, you may go." Winn thoughtfully considered the unusual call for a few moments, knowing she should write on her scroll and not keep the other ministers waiting. But she couldn't imagine why Deanna Troi would make contact with her. They had met only once, at the Alliance gathering that had chosen Kira Nerys to become Intendant of Bajor.

Winn pressed the panel, letting the screen rise from the back of her desk. She accessed the message banks and activated the return sequence. It took only a few moments for Deanna Troi to appear on the screen. The woman's hair was immaculately curled and piled on top of her head, with clusters of ringlets falling to her shoulders. Her dark, smoldering eyes fastened on Winn, and the older woman was glad that the empath could not sense her uneasiness through the subspace channel.

"First Minister Winn," Troi acknowledged in her beautifully accented voice. "Thank you for calling me back so soon."

"To what do I owe this honor, Intendant?" Winn asked politely.

Troi leaned forward. "Do you mind if I secure this transmission?"

Winn's brow lifted. "Is that necessary?"

"I believe so. I do not have faith in the Bajoran Intendant."

"You believe Kira Nerys may be monitoring my transmissions?"

Troi laughed lightly. "Not just yours. Every transmission going in and out of Bajoran territory."

Winn knew that if she protested the accusation and supported Kira's integrity, then Troi could not betray her to the Intendant. Yet this could be an opening to test her allegiance to Kira. Winn figured everyone knew about the enmity that lay between the Intendant of Bajor and the First Minister.

"Kira is capable of anything," Winn agreed, allowing the transmission to be scrambled. That would also prevent either side from recording what was said. Winn was willing to speak off the record with Troi.

Troi looked at her carefully for a moment, through

the telltale lines of scramble static on the screen. "You don't like Kira, do you?"

"Like her? That's unimportant." Winn waited for Troi to get to the point.

Troi toyed with a ringlet. "I wouldn't like the woman who had killed my mentor in order to gain the post of Intendant."

Winn heard her own voice go icy. "I see the rumors about Opaka's death have traveled far. However, Kira was absolved of the charge of assassination while she was still chief of security on Terok Nor."

"We know the truth behind that decision. It merely proved Kira had a majority of the Bajoran ministers on her payroll."

"That was over five years ago." Despite her anger, Winn spoke evenly. She would not betray her feelings for Opaka, whom she had served as devotedly as Ziyal now served her. "If you thought she was a murderer, why didn't you say anything before she was confirmed as Intendant?"

"I didn't know it then." Troi shrugged, a graceful lift of her leather-clad shoulder. "I voted against her anyway. I do not trust Kira. But now she controls every Intendant in the Alliance, and she will only grow more domineering and incorrigible. Do you want that for Bajor?"

Winn didn't need to be reminded of the danger of Kira's new post as Overseer. Bajor was already being subsumed by the Alliance, with nothing to show for it. "Everything you say is true. But what can I do about it?"

"You are in a better position than anyone to do something about it." Troi glanced down. "Perhaps it is time Kira paid for the death of Opaka. Then it would only be natural for the Alliance to name the alternate candidate, First Minister Winn, as Intendant of the Bajoran territory . . ."

Winn felt a leap of hope in spite of herself. "The case against Kira has already been closed in the Bajoran courts."

"What is the punishment if Kira is found guilty of assassinating Opaka?"

"That would be high treason. Death is the penalty."

Troi again played with a ringlet of hair, twining it around one finger. "Justice is served in many ways. Not always through the courts."

Winn was certain she had never heard assassination discussed so delicately. But Troi couldn't have been more plain if she had said, "Kill Kira Nerys and you will become Intendant." "How can I be certain that someone else, perhaps that Cardassian Gul Dukat, would not become Intendant of Bajor?"

"I will make sure of that," Troi pledged. "I know who my allies are. The other Intendants will be so happy to have the Overseer eliminated that they will approve the first person put forward for Bajor. But it has to be done quickly, otherwise the post of Overseer will become ingrained in the Alliance."

"I see." Winn felt slightly dazed. She would give almost anything to be Intendant of Bajor. She would be able to fight the Alliance from the most powerful position in the Bajoran sector. But could she kill Kira in order to get it? Could she be brought that low?

"Proceed quickly," Troi warned before signing off.

Winn remained seated at the desk, staring at the walls

without seeing. Her people were dying every day at the Romulan front. As Intendant, Winn could cut the conscription quotas. The death of one woman would serve millions of Bajorans. Besides, didn't Kira Nerys deserve to die?

Ziyal politely knocked, then said through the door, "First Minister, the ministers asked me to—"

"Yes, yes," Winn replied. "I'm coming."

Hastily, she scribbled "Kira Nerys" on her Renewal Scroll and rolled it up. Kira was certainly her biggest problem right now.

Winn composed herself as she led the way into the courtyard where the braziers were blazing. The other ministers fell in behind her, followed by the assistants and administrators.

Winn felt as if her guilt was written on her face. She was going to become a murderer to save them all. She could hardly look at the rosy-faced foster children, knowing she had forever lost her own innocence.

Yet as she laid the scroll on the burning coals, letting the fire lick up the sides of the white parchment, she could almost see the name of Kira Nerys charring black and disintegrating into ashes. Yes, it could be that easy. One stroke and her troubles would be over. It was the first necessary step in destroying the Alliance that held her people in thrall.

Later that night, when the ministers and their families had returned to their homes, Winn Adami continued to sit at her desk considering Troi's proposition. She tried to tell herself that it was impossible, remembering Circle meetings at which she had forbidden any mention of using violence to gain their goal. But her decision had been made.

Winn activated a secret channel straight to her primary contact in the Circle. She would place the matter in Leeta's hands, telling her everything and urging the Circle to take action against Kira. Winn didn't know Leeta's family name or where she had come from before joining the Circle, but the First Minister had learned to trust the valiant woman. Leeta would take care of everything.

Chapter 12

LEETA SIGNED OFF with Jadzia, the Trill who was her black-market contact, after getting the location of the rendezvous site. Jadzia had told her that a mercenary would meet her in the main bar on Bajor XII. Jadzia was a disreputable person Leeta had maintained contact with for just such occasions. But Leeta didn't trust Jadzia enough to tell her the specifics of the contract. She simply requested a mercenary who could do "unusual" jobs.

Leeta was glad Winn Adami had finally come to her senses. Perhaps it had helped that Leeta had argued for the past year that stronger measures were needed. Now the Circle could make some progress. The complacent Bajorans who grew fat under the Alliance called the members of the Circle terrorists, but Leeta knew they were freedom fighters. They also had plenty of local support. After three generations of fighting Romulans, everyone had lost a brother, mother, friend, or lover at the front.

Leeta's current mission would be the next step in breaking the Alliance's bloody grip on Bajor. Most recently, the Circle had gained the support of a few key ministers, including Winn. Leeta remembered her first meeting with Winn after the First Minister made overtures to the Circle. She had gone to Winn's house with donations of clothing for the revolving pack of orphans the kind old woman supported. Winn had spoken anxiously about the death tolls and loss of precious resources, but she had been reassured by Leeta's insistence that Bajor must be autonomous from the Alliance. Apparently the First Minister's conscience had bothered her, as if she feared she was being disloyal to her people.

But now First Minister Winn had finally agreed that Kira Nerys must be eliminated. Leeta was thrilled. She had been kept out of every interesting covert operation since becoming Winn's contact. She couldn't afford to be linked to the Circle when she was meeting with Winn. So she had spent nearly two standard years trying to convince Winn to do even the smallest things to help the Circle. Now her hard work was paying off.

Leeta had kept very quiet about Winn's chance to become Intendant, informing only Li Nalas and Minister Jaro Essa, the two leaders of the Circle, to get their approval for the operation. They saw the coming darkness under Overseer Kira, and were prepared to do whatever it took to stop her from crushing Bajor with her insatiable greed. They had to get rid of Kira now, in order to take advantage of Troi's pledge to appoint Winn as the next Intendant. Then the Circle's goal to slip the hold of the Alliance could be realized.

Leeta set course for Bajor XII, and the runabout banked and headed for the outer system. It wasn't long before she noticed something on the sensor grid. She switched to manual flight operation, bypassing the computer control.

"Automatic pilot has been disengaged," the computer informed them.

"What are you doing?" Ziyal asked, turning in the copilot's seat.

In order to get to Bajor XII, Leeta had requested help from Tora Ziyal, one of Winn's administrators. Although young, Ziyal was absolutely loyal to Winn and had the necessary travel permits to perform her courier duties. Since becoming Overseer, Kira had clamped down on travel in the system to maintain security.

"See that blip on sensors?" Leeta was too busy verifying their position and supervising flight operations to lift her hands from the panel. "I'm betting that's one of the Intendant's patrols. It just came from around that moon."

Ziyal focused sensors to try to get a better reading. "You're right. It's a class-three vessel, seven crew members on board."

Leeta veered into the Denorios Belt and began weaving through the asteroids. One chunk of rock whipped by overhead, while a pitted moonlet tumbled off their port bow. Ziyal braced herself but didn't say a word. The air got moist and hot inside the small vessel from the tension. The runabout was nearly twice as old as Leeta, but it was reliable.

Leeta placed the runabout on semi-autopilot, allowing the computer to take over the complex tracking of the asteroid movements. She merely gave the helm an occasional nudge to shift their direction. She was putting their lives in danger because she wanted to avoid the patrols that cruised Bajoran space. Leeta had been provided with enough latinum to pay off the pirates, but she preferred to try to get through unnoticed. The Circle needed every slip to continue their subversive acts against the Alliance.

"Leaving the Denorios Belt," Ziyal announced. The young woman had been disturbed when Leeta explained that they needed to hire someone to kill Kira. But as soon as Ziyal realized Winn approved and would benefit from it, she stopped asking questions. Ziyal knew nothing about the Circle.

"That should do it," Leeta said. "I'm setting a new course for Bajor XII—"

They both saw the patrol cruiser emerging from the asteroid belt.

"How did they follow us?" Ziyal exclaimed.

Leeta quickly powered down engines, knowing they couldn't outrun the patrol on impulse. They also couldn't go to warp unless they were outside the system. She couldn't risk having the cruiser fire on their engines, but she left shields raised to prevent a boarding party from joining them.

"Get ready," Leeta told Ziyal. "You may have to cover for us."

Leeta answered the patrol's hail and spoke to the captain of the aptly named *Denorios*, Benjamin Sisko. As she figured, the pirate wanted them to pay a "duty" for passing through the area.

Leeta had encountered Captain Sisko before, and she used her smile and dimples to disarm the tense situation. Sisko's expression was fierce because she had forced him to chase her. But Leeta just giggled and said it was more exciting that way.

Leeta almost had him. She had been told by other members of the Circle that she was "too cute" to be a terrorist. Usually her feminine charms worked to her advantage. But before she could approve the transfer of credit from her account to pay the duty, Sisko was informed by his second-in-command that the runabout had not filed a flight plan.

Leeta hadn't been able to file a flight plan because Jadzia had refused to give her the location of the rendezvous until after they had left Bajor. Apparently the mercenary was skittish.

If there was anything Sisko liked more than a pretty woman, it was money. He leaned forward, smelling a chance to extort more from her. "Where are you going that's so secret?"

"I'm just the pilot," Leeta denied. "Perhaps you should speak to my passenger."

Leeta turned the screen to Ziyal and let her take over. This was exactly the reason her superiors in the Circle had suggested she ask for Ziyal's help.

"I am Tora Ziyal, Third Assistant to First Minister Winn." Ziyal looked very young to sound so sure of herself. "Our flight plan to Bajor XII was filed with Bajoran Central within the past hour. You should have it in your database . . ."

Leeta smiled at Sisko's bluster as his crew tried to verify whether this was indeed Tora Ziyal. Sisko recognized her, having encountered her during her courier duties. But he went through the formality of a voice recognition and retina scan.

Leeta was glad Ziyal was with her. The young woman was like a daughter to Winn Adami, having been raised by her since she was an orphaned child. Winn had been reluctant to let Ziyal go with Leeta, but she agreed rather than hear more about their plans. Leeta knew it was weakness that made Winn avoid knowing the details, as if she would not be truly responsible for the death of another being because she wasn't actively participating in the deed.

Leeta didn't mind being responsible. When a person violated every reasonable humane tenet, then it was time to remove her from her position of power. But she was glad that Winn abhorred bloodshed. The fact boded well for Bajor under her rule. The kindly old woman had become First Minister after Opaka had been murdered because no one else was brave or foolish enough to take the post.

Even though Sisko couldn't locate their flight plan, and he probably knew one had never been filed, he was reluctant to interfere with an assistant to the First Minister of Bajor. After reminding Ziyal that even the First Minister must obey the rules established by the Intendant, Sisko finally let them go. After all, he was only a petty thief, and he didn't want to get caught in the middle of a feud between Kira and Winn. He probably wouldn't even report their encounter, which suited Leeta perfectly.

Leeta winked at Sisko as she signed off, glad to get one over on Kira and her minions. Then she set course for Bajor XII.

Leeta was waiting in the bar with Ziyal on Bajor XII when she saw the mercenary. Her eyes opened wide in admiration. Jadzia had warned Leeta that the mercenary was "something else," but she couldn't believe her eyes. The mercenary looked Bajoran, with her wrinkled nose bridge and thick reddish-brown hair, but there was something exotic about her. Her bulky jumper barely hid her curvaceous body, and her bearing and grace caught everyone's attention in the bar. Several patrons appreciatively watched her stroll through the bar, yet she didn't seem to notice them.

Uncertain if this was indeed the mercenary, Leeta flashed a subtle hand signal. The woman flicked her small finger in response. It was the correct signal.

"You must be Leeta," the woman said as she arrived at their table. "Call me Mabrin—"

Leeta didn't want anyone noticing them or Ziyal, who had her hood pulled up around her head to conceal her Cardassian features. Though the bar was filled with aliens, there were also Bajorans who might get curious about such an outstanding woman.

So Leeta jumped up and flung her arms around the mercenary. "Play along," Leeta whispered. The woman seemed startled, but she held still.

"Darling!" Leeta exclaimed. "It's so good to see you again."

The mercenary was stiff in her embrace, but her hands tentatively patted Leeta's back. Her voice was low, "I almost pulled my knife on you—"

Leeta planted a kiss right on her full lips. She gave the astonished woman a grin. "Now they know you're spoken for."

Indeed, as the two women seated themselves, the other patrons in the bar appeared to have lost interest. The mercenary was frowning, her eyes shifting away from Leeta.

"Sorry about that," Leeta told her, but she didn't really feel sorry.

Meanwhile Ziyal was busy examining the area with her microscanner, to be sure that they weren't being recorded or holo-imaged. Leeta waited patiently until Ziyal put the scanner away, then she checked to make sure the shadow over Ziyal's face was too dark to allow the mercenary to see her.

"Here is the countersign Jadzia gave me," the mercenary told Leeta, sliding a disc forward.

Leeta quickly ran it through her padd, getting a confirmation. It was the same one they had sent to Jadzia. She nodded at Ziyal, who finally relaxed, sitting back in her chair. The young woman took care to pull her hood even farther over her face.

Thoughtfully, Leeta removed the disc. "Jadzia told me that you might be able to help us, though it may be out of your typical line of work."

"What do you want?" the woman asked bluntly.

Ziyal spoke up for the first time. "How do we know you won't inform on us?"

"I'm a professional. I obtain business from satisfied customers like Jadzia." She didn't seem bothered by her faceless questioner.

Leeta nodded. Jadzia said the mercenary tended to perform "unorthodox" jobs.

"If you wish to cancel our negotiations—" the mercenary started to say.

"No, I'm just not sure you would want this job." Leeta felt somewhat uncertain. The woman's name definitely wasn't Mabrin. And something about her wasn't quite right. She appeared to be wearing a wig that was too dark for her pale skin and brows. What if she was a spy from Kira herself? But there was no way around it. "It's a contract on Kira Nerys."

"The new Overseer?" The mercenary glanced away as if she couldn't believe she had gone out of her way for this. "You can't be serious."

"No, and here's the latinum to prove it." Leeta slid the padd forward.

The mercenary didn't pick it up at first, but Leeta urged her to go ahead. Her eyes widened when she read the enormous credit balance on the padd, checking it again to be sure. Several mercenaries could retire on the amount. It was attached to a contract waiting for her thumbprint to transfer the balance to a secured account, payment to be made upon the completion of the job.

Leeta was pleased to see her aloof demeanor crack. Now she wasn't acting like they were a couple of backwater rubes.

"You're serious?" the mercenary asked again.

"Absolutely. But it must be done by Stardate 47104.0, payment in full on the death of the Intendant. Otherwise the secured latinum will be sent to a Bajoran charity. If you try to abscond with the money, they will track you down."

Leeta had to smile, thinking about the strength of the Bajoran Veterans League. Nobody in their right mind would try to steal from them. But the Circle had managed to route an enormous donation to the Bajoran Veterans League through their banking center. It gave them a few weeks to manipulate the latinum. If the assassination worked, Winn would become Overseer with almost unlimited credit at her disposal, and they could pay the BVL with no one being the wiser. If she didn't complete the job, then the latinum would still go to the BVL. Nice and neat.

The mercenary read the entire contract again. It was as airtight as a legal document could get. Except it left the specifications of the exact job to a "rider" to be verbally confirmed.

Leeta pulled another padd from her pocket. "If the job is too much for you, then simply refuse. We offer you another contract. You don't say a word about this, and in a standard year you will get a smaller sum of latinum."

The mercenary didn't bother looking at the second padd. "If I accept, may I complete the contract on my own terms? Without interference from you?"

"You won't have any contact with us unless you need our assistance. I'll give you the necessary information to reach me."

"Very well." The mercenary placed her thumb against the screen of the padd. "I accept."

On the way back to Bajor, Leeta felt slightly let down. She didn't talk to Ziyal, who was similarly withdrawn. It was a terrible thing they had done, but Leeta was determined to see it through. She would have liked more assurance from the mercenary that the job would get done, but in another way, her rigid detachment was convincing in itself. Surely a woman like that would be able to handle Kira Nerys.

Chapter 13

AGENT SEVEN RETURNED to her shuttlecraft and departed Major XII. Once she was outside the system, she relayed a message to Enabran Tain to contact her on a secured channel.

Seven didn't know if Tain would order her to fulfill the contract on Kira she had just accepted. It didn't matter to her. It wasn't her latinum that would go to the Bajoran veterans if she didn't do the job.

Agent Seven took the shuttlecraft deep into the neighboring sector while waiting for Tain to respond. In the distance, the Badlands stretched as far as the eye could see, a ruddy orange and gold mass of plasma storms. Blue discharge bolts danced along the outer edges. The major shipping lanes were routed around this sector because of the danger.

Seven was perfectly content to wait as long as it took for Tain to respond. Meanwhile she monitored sensor

data on the Badlands and the few brief indicators o
other ships that appeared on long-range sensors. Now
that she was back on duty, even if it was only limited
duty, nothing else mattered.

She had chafed at her prolonged vacation. Her face
was still too fragile for physical alteration. But for her
rendezvous with Leeta, Seven had applied the Bajoran
nose bridge in spite of her doctor's orders to stay away
from the mobile surgical unit. She hated wearing her
own face and couldn't resist changing it to something
else.

While she completed her recovery, Tain had ordered
her to cruise the sectors adjacent to Bajor and to observe
the level of activity in the various systems while avoiding direct contact with other starships. Bajor was a high
priority with the Obsidian Order because Kira Nerys
had been named Overseer. No one knew exactly what
effect that would have, but everyone suspected it would
shake things up.

So when Jadzia had left a message on their contact
frequency, Agent Seven had been in the area to respond
immediately. She didn't think it would involve something as critical as this; therefore, she hadn't bothered to
clear the rendezvous with Tain. She was certain Jadzia
didn't know the details of the contract. Jadzia didn't get
involved in murder. She often claimed the best way to
lose your freedom was to commit a capital offense.

Agent Seven was aware she might be disciplined for
minor infractions such as using the mobile surgical unit
and making contact with Leeta without proper notifica-
tion. Yet when Tain returned her call, she didn't let that

knowledge affect her report. She informed Tain of the contract and the terms that had been offered to her.

"My implant contains an image of the Bajoran woman called Leeta," Seven finished. "The other contact was shadowed the entire time. However, I detected certain Cardassian inflections in her voice."

"Interesting . . . So a Cardassian wants to assassinate Kira Nerys," Tain said speculatively.

"The probability is sixty-seven percent," Seven replied. "However, I obtained an image of the woman's hands. They are clearly not Cardassian."

"Both women could have been physically altered," Tain pointed out.

Seven knew that was true. Yet she was also experienced at detecting individuals who didn't conform to their species' behavior patterns. Leeta had been saturated with Bajoran characteristics, while the other one . . . She was different.

Tain rubbed his mouth, considering the information. "Infiltrate Kira's associates, and act as if you are complying with the contract. I want more information about the source. Find out who that other woman is, and who instigated this plan."

"Very well." Seven restated her orders, to be sure she understood correctly. "I am to comply with my contract while making further contact with Leeta and the unknown woman."

"Yes, and find out more about our new Overseer while you're at it." Tain lifted a warning finger. "But don't harm her."

"Understood. I will need information on Kira Nerys."

"Yes . . ." Tain was saying, as if to himself. "This may work out very well. I have a way you can get close to Kira. But you'll need to get rid of that nose. You'll have to appear Terran for it to work."

"Terran?" Seven was taken aback.

"Yes, Kira never lets anyone get close to her except her Terran slaves."

Seven's cool poise broke. "I don't want to look Terran."

Tain looked at her more closely, clearly intrigued by her refusal. "I think that's the first time you've ever said no to me."

"I . . . *Ser*, I didn't intend . . ." She took a deep breath.

Tain looked as if he understood all too well. "I have your doctor's report here." Tain tapped his desk. "You were told not to apply that nose bridge. After this assignment is completed, you will have to undergo grafts to return sensation to that part of your face."

Seven didn't care if her entire body went numb. She didn't want to walk around wearing her own face. It was bad enough hiding behind a tiny nose bridge.

"You either go Terran," Tain said flatly, "or return to medical duty until you're fully recovered. I'll send another agent." Dull, useless medical duty. A fate worse than Terran slavery.

"That will not be necessary." Seven willed herself to stay expressionless. "I will complete this mission."

"Good," Tain told her. "You can expect a burst transmission containing the intelligence file we have on Kira Nerys. I'll include your instructions on the infiltration."

* * *

The next day, Seven arrived on Jeraddo, the Class-M moon in orbit around Bajor. Her nose bridge had been bobbed and the brown wig was gone. She was nakedly Terran. She avoided looking in reflective surfaces, preferring to maintain the mental image of herself as Bajoran.

The fifth moon of Bajor was a dusty, forbidding place, farmed by a few dozen hearty souls. Tain had informed her that the Bajoran ministers, on the recommendation of Intendant Kira, had agreed to tap the moon's molten core. The project would transfer large amounts of power to cities on the surface of Bajor. With resources on Bajor depleted, the new source of energy was vitally important. However, tapping the core would also release sulfur and carbon compounds into Jeraddo's atmosphere, rendering it uninhabitable. The residents of the moon would have to be evacuated.

The intelligence brief on the infiltration had included notes on the political complexities of the situation. In a handful of days, Seven would have to convince the residents of Jeraddo to resist the evacuation. The key was to create enough of a movement to attract the Intendant's personal notice without jeopardizing Seven's own life.

Agent Seven crash-landed her nondescript shuttlecraft several klicks from a small enclave of Bajorans and Free-Terrans. When they found her, she claimed that her ship had been damaged in the Denorios Belt. While she tried to "repair" her shuttlecraft, she accepted their meager hospitality and freely shared water from her replicator to gain their confidence. Once they were assured that she wasn't an escaped slave, they accepted her for her supplies if nothing else.

Luckily, there was already a resistance movement underway, led by several old Bajoran farmers. Mullibok, Keena, and Baltrim were loud in their denouncement of Intendant Kira. Seven encouraged the Terrans to join the Bajorans in resisting evacuation. Before the enforcers arrived and made a physical confrontation inevitable, Seven also encouraged the residents to contact Intendant Kira and ask her to come to the moon to arbitrate the matter.

The residents of Jerrado sent Kira a joint petition protesting the actions of the local enforcers in regard to the evacuation, emphasizing that only Kira's presence could resolve the situation. Seven made sure the petition was carefully worded, intending for Kira to read between the lines and assume that the Bajoran enforcers were mismanaging the job and deliberately creating delays for the project. She wanted Kira to wonder whether the local enforcers were under orders from the minority ministers who denounced this drastic measure with Bajor's fifth moon.

Mullibok cooperated because he had his own plan for Kira's arrival. The Bajorans wanted piles of latinum in exchange for their scrappy moon, and they were ready to threaten the Intendant to get it.

However, most of the residents wisely fled Jeraddo when they heard Kira was transporting down to the moon. The three Bajoran leaders and a handful of farmers stayed, gambling that they could better their lives. Seven was among them.

Their naïveté was breathtaking. Seven knew they were lucky the orbital patrol didn't simply blow their encampment away and end the stalemate. But Kira desperately needed this project, and she had endured personal attacks by the ministers to get their cooperation. Kira would be looking for a conspiracy.

The situation on Jerrado changed as soon as Kira materialized in the enclave. She glanced around with disdain, shielding her eyes against the wind-blown dirt. Her guards held three laser cannons pointed at the residents of Jeraddo, and suddenly their makeshift shelters seemed a laughable defense.

Seven stepped forward, ignoring the constant wind that had reddened her eyes and cheeks over the past few days. Her layers of clothing protected her from the stinging sand, but she pulled the cloth down from her mouth and neck to let Kira get a good look at her. The physician had told her that her beauty index for a Terran was in the top 1 percent of the population. That had surprised Seven. Her reaction to her own face was one of revulsion. However, Tain's information had emphasized that Kira appreciated attractive Terrans.

Guards immediately stepped forward to stop Seven from approaching Kira. The Intendant hardly deigned to notice her.

In some ways, Kira Nerys reminded Seven of Enabran Tain. The slight, red-haired woman cast an oppressive cloud over the assembled rebels, who hardly moved when she appeared. Suddenly they were all aware that at the slightest provocation, Kira's guards would open fire. She obviously had the ability to destroy people and property on a whim.

Kira turned to the group of moon farmers gathered on

the dirt in front of Mullibok's home. "Why do you people resist the evacuation?" Kira raised her voice to carry over the wind. "You're delaying a vital project that will bring power to millions of Bajorans."

"And *we* lose everything!" Mullibok called. He was an older Bajoran with a sparse fringe of hair on his head. But he was strong from fighting the desiccated fields on the moon. He stepped to the front of the crowd, but not as far forward as Seven. "I've farmed this land for forty years, poured my life into it. What compensation can you give us that will make up for that?"

"Do not trust this man," Seven quickly told Kira. "There are two phaser rifles trained on you from those rocks—"

The guards leaped into action. Seven was immediately slammed to the ground facedown, with a knee in her back. The farmers began to cry out in terror as the guards surrounded them. Kira was instantly protected by three guards who closed to form a shield around her. At least a dozen more guards immediately transported down to the planet at various dispersal points, expertly clearing out the rocks and searching the enclave. Phaser shots were fired, and the high whine of a laser cannon was followed by several explosions.

Seven couldn't see a thing with her face in the dirt, but the screams from Keena indicated that her partner, Baltrim, had been killed during the skirmish.

Seven could have easily disabled the guard on her back, but her careful analysis of Kira's character profile indicated that she liked to be magnanimous to Terrans who were in trouble. She waited patiently, knowing that now Kira would be curious about her.

Indeed, once the rebel gunners were taken into custody, Kira ordered the guard to drag Seven closer. Rough hands hauled her up, and she found her feet with difficulty, wiping the dust from her eyes and mouth.

As Kira stepped closer, Seven kept her hands out from her sides to calm the guards. She was Terran, and vulnerable in a way she hadn't felt since she was very young.

Kira's short red hair was blown about in the wind. "Why did you betray your friends?" Kira's tone was no longer reasonable, and her hands were on her hips. She was angry that the farmers had set a trap for her.

"They are not my friends," Seven replied evenly. "I crash-landed on this moon several days ago. That's when I discovered their plan."

From among the six remaining farmers, now prisoners surrounded by guards, Mullibok began shouting, "Spy! It's all your fault. I'll kill you—"

The guards were moving the farmers to a beam-out point. At Kira's gesture, each guard took a prisoner in custody for the transport to the ore reclamation unit on Terok Nor. Seven carefully kept her eyes on Kira.

Kira turned back to Seven. "Where's your vessel?"

"That second ridge." Seven pointed to the dip in the nearby hills. "The power transfer conduits overloaded in the Denorios Belt, and my ship crashed. One of the warp nacelles is damaged. I've been replicating new conduits and was attempting to repair the impulse drive when I encountered these farmers."

Kira jerked her head at one of her guards to check out

her story. The guard beamed away, presumably to the second ridge to find the shuttlecraft.

Finally Kira took a closer look at Seven, circling the taller woman. Seven lifted her chin, enduring Kira's scrutiny. This was the moment she had worked so hard to bring about.

"Who are you?" Kira demanded.

Seven hesitated. "Annika Hansen. I'm a merchant pilot out of Yridia." Tain had provided the cover story and created the contacts necessary to confirm it. "I'm transporting a load of microbiotic material to the Bajoran Cybernetic Institute. They are probably wondering why I'm late."

Kira shook her head, irritated by the constant sand flying through the air. "You're lying. That's not your real name."

Seven was astonished at herself for hesitating. It was the first lesson they learned in the training facility. But instinctively she rejected the use of her true name. "That is who I am. You can check the registration of my shuttlecraft."

Kira waved her away, no longer interested. With the sure instincts of a master deceiver, she knew Seven was lying. "Registrations are easily altered. Security will have to deal with you. Take her to ore reclamation."

Kira was starting to leave, letting her guards take over. Seven couldn't lose this chance to make an impression on Kira.

"Don't go!" she called after Kira, dragging the guards a few steps. If only the wind would stop howling between them. "My friends have a nickname for me, but it is . . . foolish. That's why I didn't tell you." She had finally caught Kira's attention.

The redhead looked back. "What is it?"

"Seven." She shrugged, trying to appear graceful while keeping her back to the blowing sand. "I almost answered 'Seven,' but I realized you would need my official designation."

Kira laughed. "You mean, like the number seven?" When Seven nodded, she asked, "How did you get such an unusual name?"

Seven's implant database had already determined the most common way individuals acquired nicknames. "My mother and older siblings called me Seven because I was the seventh child. I didn't have a name until I went to school."

"So you've always been a Free-Terran," Kira said speculatively.

"Yes." Seven pushed her point. "I could not allow the farmers to harm the Intendant of Bajor. I'm a loyal subject of the Alliance."

"I see," Kira said approvingly.

At that moment, the guard returned and reported to Kira that a shuttlecraft had indeed crashed nearby and was in need of repairs. There was a load of cryogenically suspended microbiotic material on board. The logs stated the shuttlecraft had left Yridia and had been due to deliver the cargo to the Cybernetic Institute. Seven trusted her background material as thoroughly as if she were indeed a minor merchant pilot.

"Smart girl," Kira told Seven. "You made the right choice."

Seven didn't respond. Her database indicated that Kira preferred to maintain absolute control. In fact, her projections for this mission indicated a 94 percent probability that Kira would make her a slave. However, that was unimportant as long as she was near Kira.

"Take this one to the *Siren's Song*," Kira ordered her guards. "Let's proceed with the tap."

Seven allowed the guards to shove her to the beam-out point. As Kira briefly conferred with another guard, she glanced once more at Seven in a speculative way. It was enough to give the agent a leap of confidence that she had played her role well.

The guard was expressionless as they transported up to the *Siren's Song*. Seven was silently escorted to a small room on board the ship. At least she hadn't been taken to ore reclamation along with the Jeraddo farmers.

Through the hours that followed, Seven patiently sat near the portal in her holding cell. Terok Nor disappeared in its orbit around Bajor, where it would be protected in case something went wrong with the core tap. Soon a tractor beam pulled her shuttlecraft up to the *Siren's Song*. The battered shuttlecraft closed in and she could see the damaged warp nacelle before it disappeared, probably into the shuttle bay.

Meanwhile, various starships gathered around Jeraddo. When the tapping began, the science vessel sent a brilliant blue-green laser boring down on the moon. The thick beam looked as though it could punch a hole through a sun, and the light made Seven squint away from the portal. But she forced herself to watch as the atmosphere of the moon darkened under the bombardment, then finally exploded as the molten core was exposed. The surface was now sterile. No living thing could survive on Jeraddo again. The laser converted the energy of the core into a sustainable beam directed down at the planet Bajor.

Agent Seven noted the competent organization. The procedure went remarkably smoothly for such a complex project. As always, Enabran Tain would appreciate the details.

Seven did not care that the moon had been destroyed. She did not worry about being in the custody of a megalomaniac who would not hesitate to kill her if her true mission was discovered. Seven felt truly alive only when she was undercover. Nothing else mattered.

Chapter 14

MODERN CARDASSIANS HAD to seize every opportunity to rise because such opportunities came few and far between. Elim Garak knew that better than anyone. His current undercover assignment for the Obsidian Order was to serve as security chief of Terok Nor. For two long years he had worked for Intendant Kira, who was suddenly now Overseer of every sector in the former Terran Empire. Garak continually marveled at that woman's ingenuity. Actually, he marveled that she was able to accomplish anything from this backwater territory. It certainly hadn't done his career any good.

So when Garak received a covert message from Enabran Tain that he should be prepared to offer Annika Hansen any assistance she required, he knew that an opportunity might be heading his way. Garak was rarely informed of agents' operations in his sector.

Garak was on hand to meet Kira when the *Siren*'

Song docked at Terok Nor after the successful tapping of Jeraddo. The new Overseer was just leaving the airlock with a striking blond Terran. The Terran's skin and eyes were reddened, and Kira laughed as the woman bent over and shook some sand out of her cuff.

"I'm glad to get away from that place," she was saying to Kira.

"Happy hunting?" Garak brightly inquired, as Kira stepped over the rim of the airlock.

"Isn't there some security detail you should be taking care of?" Kira retorted, her delight momentarily interrupted.

"Nothing more important than the return of my Overseer," Garak responded, light on the sarcasm. Their animosity had settled into a practiced, barbed repartee. Reasonable people would agree that Kira should have tried to form an alliance with him, and it was frustrating that she rejected his every offer of assistance. Then again, Kira had done quite well for herself . . . so far.

Kira ignored Garak, tucking her hand under the Terran's arm. "This way, my dear."

"You've brought back a visitor?" Garak gave the woman a sweeping once-over. She had a trim, powerful body, and was turning as if prepared to strike without warning. Obviously a trained Obsidian assassin.

Garak met her eyes with particular emphasis, but Annika Hansen didn't betray herself with a flicker of recognition. She undoubtedly had been briefed that he was a fellow Obsidian Order agent, but she was like stone. Impressed, Garak glanced at Kira. "I don't suppose this young woman will need quarters."

"I'll take care of it," Kira said with a smug smile. "You're dismissed."

Garak was left behind as Kira sauntered down the curved corridor of the docking ring, her slinky stride unmistakable in the midst of her servants. Annika was different from the others, wary but not subservient.

The confidential tilt of Kira's head as she talked to Annika made Garak smile smugly. Enabran Tain was using information that Garak himself had gathered. Garak had long believed the best way to get an agent close to Kira was to play on her capricious sensual appetite. Obviously he had been correct. A beautiful Terran was the key.

Garak went back to his security office and immediately returned a message to Enabran Tain, acknowledging the arrival of Annika Hansen. He assured the head of the Obsidian Order that he would "keep an eye on her."

Garak intended to please Tain by promptly complying with his orders, but that evening he received another message from Tain. Garak felt an unaccustomed leap of eagerness at the sight of the Obsidian Order insignia.

It was an encrypted communiqué, and Garak impatiently ran it through the program on his personal padd. The head and shoulders of Enabran Tain appeared on the tiny screen. Garak had just enough time to note with dismay the deepening wrinkles around his father's eyes and jowls before Tain spoke.

The old man ordered, "Leave her alone, Garak. If I find you've interfered with her, you will regret it. Tain out."

"Ungrateful tyrant," Garak muttered, leaning back in his cushioned command chair in the Security Office

His desk curved in front of him, suddenly reminding him of his father's command station in the bunker on Cardassia Prime. Why had he never noticed that before? It always felt comfortable to him, this double curve of monitors and controls, and now he understood why.

Tain had never publicly acknowledged that Garak was his son, and only a few people were aware of it. Garak wouldn't have minded as much if Tain had privately acknowledged their relationship, but he didn't. It was as if Garak had stopped being Tain's son after his mother had left the old man.

Yet even before that, his father had never hidden his disdain for his own son. Garak knew he had been posted on Terok Nor to keep him away from Gul Dukat, after he had successfully—and brilliantly, he might add—implicated Dukat's father in criminal activities. As a reward, Garak had been cooling his heels on this dull station for the best years of his life. When Gul Dukat stepped down as Intendant, most of the other Cardassians had also left. He was practically living in exile because he had done as his father ordered.

Tain had never thanked him, never even acknowledged that he had done a good job. Garak slammed his fist down on the desk.

"Sir?" a security guard asked, on his way through the office to the brig.

"Nothing," Garak said, shrugging off his irritation with the ease of years of practice. There was no use getting upset about it. Now he had to figure out how to make the best of the situation.

He passed his fingers over the controls and activated

the security monitors in Kira's reception room. Kira wouldn't dare allow Annika Hansen into her private quarters until her security checks were completed. Surely the Obsidian Order had done their job and Kira's people would discover that Annika was merely a mercenary pilot flying an antiquated ship by permit of the Yridian empire.

Garak decided it was time to find out more about the agent posing as Annika Hansen. Who was she that his father was so anxious to protect her? Just because Garak was stuck in Bajoran territory, that didn't mean he lacked contacts. He wouldn't sit by and let his father run him over. Garak had already given enough to that old man. Now he was watching out for himself.

As Garak put out feelers about the Obsidian Order agent, he continued to watch through the network of security cameras while Kira toyed with Annika. He had to admit, the agent was adept at intriguing Kira.

For two days Kira kept the agent in her public reception room waiting for the background checks to clear. She kept calling her Seven, for reasons Garak couldn't fathom. But when Garak got his first batch of information on the agent, he was appalled to see her official designation was Agent Seven of Corps Nine. He wondered what had gone wrong: Why was she being called Seven instead of Annika Hansen?

Everything else appeared to be proceeding perfectly. As Garak had suggested, the agent did not appear to be impressed by the opulent furnishings or the elaborate culinary delights supplied round the clock by the cooks and serving slaves. Most people were awed by the Intendant's lifestyle, but Seven acted as if it was nothing unusual. Garak had suggested the tactic in his reports after watching Benjamin Sisko's careless attitude toward material things. Sisko was far more interested in playing the game than winning profits, and Kira was more lenient and generous with him than with anyone else.

Kira lolled on a sofa, letting one of her slave girls place a sugared stardust puff in her mouth. Seven was at the computer terminal, trying to get clearance to deliver her cargo of microbiotic material to the Bajoran Cybernetic Institute. Apparently Seven was caught up in bureaucratic red tape, having missed her assigned delivery date. She exhibited signs of frustration as the screen returned to the Cybernetic Institute logo. Her request to make delivery was being routed to another office.

Over her shoulder, Seven told Kira, "It is unfortunate that my power systems overloaded *before* I was able to make delivery."

"Unfortunate for you, perhaps." Kira slowly smiled. "Then again, perhaps not."

Seven inclined her head. "Perhaps not."

Garak found himself leaning closer to the surveillance display, murmuring his approval. Seven was behaving exactly as he had suggested in his reports. The way to get close to Kira was to retreat and let Kira pursue. Kira didn't care about anyone who wanted her, and she could sense desire a light-year away. Garak knew that was one reason Kira continually rejected his overtures. He wanted her goodwill too much because he was powerless in his current post unless she worked with him. But the woman was mean and suspicious and intent on pleasing only herself.

He focused the screen in closer as Kira sat up, a frown line forming between her brows. She waved the slave girl off. "You sound like you'd rather not be here."

Obviously aware of the other people in the room, Seven quietly replied, "I survive through my work."

"Didn't anyone ever teach you to take the opportunities that fall into your lap?" Kira swung her feet off the chaise and sat up. "You're acting positively ungrateful that I saved you from that moon."

Seven glanced down at her clasped hands. "How do you want me to act?"

Garak wasn't surprised to see Kira's mood abruptly change. She was mercurial, especially when she was testing a new person. Kira laughed. "Just be yourself. I hate pretense."

The agent didn't seem bothered by the contradiction, scoring another point in Garak's opinion. *"This* is who I am," Seven told her. "You are not the first to say I'm not . . . warm and accessible. I'm cautious, just as you are."

Even through the surveillance monitor, Garak could hear the sincerity in her voice. He believed her, and apparently so did Kira. While Kira was charmed by her cool demeanor, Garak was unpleasantly reminded of his father—a cold, unfeeling automaton. This agent was too good, too perfect. Despite the fact that they were on the same side, he didn't trust her.

The computer screen beeped, drawing Seven's attention back to her "work." A brisk Bajoran in a lab coat told her, "*You missed your delivery date, Captain Hansen. We will not need resupply for thirty days. If you would like to contract now for resupply, that is acceptable. But one more missed delivery, and the Bajoran Cybernetic Institute will no longer ship through your line.*"

"Understood," Seven said. "I will complete the delivery in thirty standard days."

"*So noted, we'll see you then, Captain.*" The Bajoran nodded as she signed off.

"See!" Kira exclaimed. "Now all you have to do is make your delivery and everything is back to normal."

"First I have to repair the warp nacelle on my shuttlecraft." Seven turned to Kira, her expression serious. "Will you allow me to stay here until the delivery?"

Garak held his breath. One could never be sure what Kira would do. She didn't like to be asked for things, but apparently she had been won over by the ice queen.

Kira held out her hand with a warm smile. "Seven, I would like nothing better than to keep you on Terok Nor for a while longer." Kira waited until the Terran came over to take her hand, sitting on the edge of the chaise. "And I know just the person who can fix your shuttlecraft."

The agent seemed to relax, her full lips curving in response. Kira leaned closer, obviously drawn to her physically.

"Excuse me, Overseer?" The majordomo, Serge, hesitated in the doorway. "You said you wanted this the nanosecond it came in—"

"Give it to me!" Kira demanded. Seven retreated as Kira snatched the padd from the majordomo's hand.

Garak assumed it was the report she had ordered on

"Annika Hansen." He shifted camera angles so he could see the agent as well. Her expression was so impassive that only an expert could tell that she was alert. Garak had spent too many hours examining his father's stoic face to miss the hint of anticipation in her eyes. She had also risen slightly on the balls of her feet, ready to react to save herself, if necessary.

Kira let her hand fall into her lap, staring off into space for a moment. Garak tensed, almost expecting it to be over. But he should have known that Enabran Tain would not allow his plan to fail.

"Come, Seven," Kira ordered, languidly rising from her chaise. "Let's go where we can be more comfortable."

Garak knew the Obsidian Order had won as Kira gestured for the agent to join her in her private quarters where there were no security cameras. He felt an ugly satisfaction that Kira was enthralled by a Cardassian. If only she knew that gray skin lay under the agent's Terran facade, she would have been appalled at herself. For some reason, Kira had a pronounced antipathy toward Cardassians.

One of Garak's contacts had sent him an image of Agent Seven as she really looked. She was a rather unattractive woman with pronounced eye ridges and thick lips. But Kira only saw Seven in her Terran guise, and according to the lingering, admiring looks she got from the other slaves, she must be considered quite appealing. Kira couldn't seem to take her eyes away as Seven crossed the room to join her.

On their way out of the reception room, Kira shot a disgusted look at the security camera. Garak felt an answering rise of bitterness. Did she think it was thrilling to watch her indulge herself with slaves and food and fine things when he had none? But he couldn't lie to himself. If he had been able to get a surveillance eye into Kira's private quarters, especially the decadently opulent pool chamber and inner sanctum, he would have watched constantly. Instead, he was left with the empty reception room.

Soon, the flurry of movement ceased, with only a serving slave left to clean up the mess. Garak continued to stare at the screen for lack of anything better to do. But it was a sad sight, the big luxurious chamber now left empty.

Surreptitiously Garak glanced at the doorway of his security office, then the other way into the brig. None of his guards were around.

Sitting back, Garak pictured himself surrounded by serving slaves and living Kira's life, with the power and influence to do what he wished. Then, from a compulsion that now came as much from physical need as his desire to forget everything, he triggered his cranial implant.

Early in his second year on Terok Nor, Garak had discovered how to trigger his cranial implant, designed to help agents resist torture and interrogation. Through a loop in the software, he had inserted a simple auto-command. It worked so well that he wondered if any other field agents on long-term assignments had discovered the trick. He felt himself falling into the blissful pool that waited for him . . .

"Ahhh," he breathed, relaxing into the chair.

As the waves of endorphins filled his body and lifted his spirit, Garak knew it was more than boredom that prompted him to forget everything in the lure of the implant. What did he have to look forward to in his life? Only the Obsidian Order and the mind-numbing repetition of his job as security chief, living alone on Terok Nor with hardly another Cardassian to talk to . . . Could anyone wonder at his desire to forget everything, even if it was only for a stolen moment?

Chapter 15

ON THE WAY to his patrol cruiser, Sisko stopped by the service bay closest to his quarters on Terok Nor. Kira had ordered all of the patrols to collect duties and maintain security, ending his crew's leave early. He had been ignoring their complaints since this morning's announcement. But that's what happened whenever the Regent visited Terok Nor. This was the second time since Kira had been made Overseer that Worf had come to Bajoran territory.

The flagship of the Alliance armada was in synchronous orbit with Terok Nor, dwarfing the station. Worf had refused to dock at one of the main pylons. He had arrived unexpectedly this time, detouring to Terok Nor after winning a huge battle against the Romulans. Everyone was saying it was the first step in an offensive that would sweep the Romulans all the way back to Romulus.

The bay door opened and Sisko swaggered in, checking out the place. The work lights were focused on a battered shuttlecraft in the middle of the service bay, but only one pair of legs were sticking out from under the vessel.

"I'll help myself," Sisko commented, moving toward the supply bins. He needed a few new power couplings for the replicators on the *Denorios*.

"Huh? Who is it?" a distinctive voice asked. There was some wiggling, then O'Brien poked his face out from under the port warp nacelle. "Oh, it's you."

Sisko was disappointed that it was only O'Brien, a Theta-class slave. Some of the Bajoran service crew would put up a fight over a few power couplings, even if Sisko was a favorite of the Intendant. O'Brien wouldn't say boo to a tweesel if it bit him on the nose.

"Don't mind if I do," Sisko drawled, reaching into the coupling bin.

O'Brien looked worried, as usual, but he didn't protest. His freckled round face was so pathetic that it irritated Sisko. It was guys like this who gave Terrans a bad name.

Just to get a rise out of him, Sisko added, "You keep smiling like that and people are gonna start asking why a slave is so happy. Maybe we should call you Smiley. How would you like that?"

Sisko took a few steps closer, clutching the four power couplings. O'Brien was silently looking at him from under the shuttlecraft, an isolinear wrench hanging slackly from his hand. If anything, he cowered deeper under the nacelle.

"Take care of these, Smiley." Sisko dropped the couplings next to the slave. "I need them calibrated for a class-three power system and delivered to my ship before Beta shift starts."

"But I have to finish these repairs! The Intendant wants it done—"

"That's Overseer to you, Smiley."

The slave swallowed, as Sisko paced down the side of the shuttlecraft, examining it.

"This is *her* ship, isn't it?" Sisko asked. The shuttlecraft was old, and it had suffered hull-crunching damage. The warp nacelle had been straightened, but dents remained in the tarnished blue-green metal as a reminder of the crash.

"Yeah, the new Free-Terran," O'Brien agreed.

Now that Sisko saw the battered ship, he couldn't reconcile it with the blond Terran. That woman didn't seem like the type to put up with an inefficient hunk of junk like this. Sisko grinned, remembering the way she had looked down her nose at him when he tried to get chummy with her in Kira's quarters. He hadn't been there since, and he wasn't sure if it was because of Seven, or whether Kira was testing him again.

Kira had been acting strange ever since he told her about the teleportation device. She had ordered him not to speak of what had happened. Even when his crew demanded to know how he had disappeared from the *Denorios,* he refused to say a word. They knew it had something to do with Kira, and that made them fear her even more. Since there was nothing Sisko could do about it, he put the entire incident out of his mind. It wasn't a conscious decision, but something instinctive linked to his very survival. He didn't question it.

Meanwhile, Sisko had been enjoying his free time in

lots of pleasant ways while Kira was otherwise occupied. He figured everyone needed a vacation now and again . . . especially from someone as demanding as Nerys.

"Hello?" a voice called from the door of the service bay. "Anybody in here?"

Sisko stepped around the shuttlecraft while O'Brien ducked out from under the warp nacelle. A slender Trill approached, her dark hair falling loose around her shoulders. Her trim pilot's jumpsuit was belted tightly around her waist and legs as if ready for flight. She had a helmet under one arm.

"Can I help you?" Sisko asked, meaning it in every way.

She came forward and was examining the shuttlecraft. "It is the same," she muttered under her breath. "I thought so."

Sisko and O'Brien exchanged a puzzled look. "Can I help you?" Sisko asked more pointedly.

She glanced from him to O'Brien under the shuttlecraft. "I'm looking for the captain of this shuttle."

Sisko grinned. "She's not here. It's just me and Smiley." He stepped forward, his hand out. "I'm Benjamin Sisko."

"Jadzia," she said, briefly shaking his hand. She seemed agitated. "Do you know where I can find her?"

Sisko restrained himself from looking up at the surveillance cameras, knowing it was possible that Garak was watching everything that happened here. The security chief had made it clear many times before that he took special care to monitor Sisko's activities.

But Sisko knew he had nothing to hide, and there was

everything to gain from learning more about the new Free-Terran. Nobody had met her before she arrived at Terok Nor.

"You know her?" Sisko asked.

Jadzia hesitated, but she obviously had no choice. "We've worked together before, and I was hoping she could help me out. I saw this shuttle listed on the docking manifest and recognized the registry number."

Sisko looked dubious. "If you're looking for a ride, this shuttle isn't going anywhere for a while."

Jadzia shook her head. "I have my own ship, the *Rogue Star*, but my disembarking permit was denied."

"Why?"

"Why should I tell you?" Jadzia countered, her blue eyes flashing defensively.

Sisko liked it. "Because I'm a friend of the Overseer."

Underneath the shuttlecraft, O'Brien snorted and deliberately turned back to his work. In a flash of irritation, Sisko wanted to kick him. But Jadzia was looking at him with new interest.

"I'm only lacking a few slips of latinum. If the portmaster could add the balance to my docking fees next time I'm at Terok Nor, then I could complete my contract and get paid."

"That's the oldest line in the book," Sisko pointed out. "I've never seen you here before, and there's no reason for you to come back."

"I don't care what you think," Jadzia retorted. "I only asked where I could find the captain of this shuttle."

Sisko narrowed his eyes, resting one dark hand on the side of the ship. "She's been moved to quarters in the habitat ring while the Regent is here. You're in luck. It's level six, Alpha-four, right around the corner."

Caught off guard, Jadzia said, "Thanks." She nodded to Sisko, then O'Brien. "Thanks a lot."

As she turned and walked away, Sisko admired her retreating form. Definitely a hot, fiery number.

"Hey," he called after her. "If your friend can't help you, come to airlock twelve. We're short a crew member. It will give you a way to earn your docking fees."

Startled by the offer, she paused in the doorway. "You mean that?"

"Just be there before the start of Beta shift. That's when we're leaving."

Jadzia shook her head. "Thanks anyway. I'm hoping I'll be on the *Rogue Star* by then."

Sisko laughed. "Sure."

The door slid shut behind her. Sisko wondered if Seven would give her the latinum she needed. There was no other way Jadzia would get her ship back. Kira never interfered when it came to the graft the docking master exacted from passing ships, as long as he passed on half of everything to her. Sisko liked Kira's system. He didn't want anyone telling him how to run his business.

But it would be interesting to see if Seven helped the Trill. Jadzia had said they "worked together." He wondered what that meant, exactly.

He realized O'Brien was looking up at him. "You move fast," the slave told him, in a not very admiring tone.

"I like warp speed better than impulse." Sisko gave

him a toothy grin, nudging one of the couplings closer to the slave. "Better get to work on these."

"But Kira told me—"

"When will you learn, Smiley?" Sisko's voice took on a hard edge. "Don't make me tell Kira I'm stuck on the station because *you* won't adjust these couplings." He paused to let that sink in. "Install them in my ship before Beta."

O'Brien bowed his head, mumbling some sort of agreement.

Sisko was laughing to himself as he left the service bay. It was almost too easy.

Shortly before Alpha shift ended, Sisko's crew were completing the cross-checks prior to disembarking Terok Nor. O'Brien was hooking up the power couplings in the main replicator bank under the flight deck. He made the final link, then lifted his servo wrench from the conduit. "You know these couplings aren't rated for a class-3 power system."

"This engine isn't rated for a class-3 power system." Sisko leaned against a nearby wall with his arms crossed. "They're Bajoran-manufactured. They won't overload the system."

O'Brien shrugged, his expression sour. "It's your funeral."

"You know, Smiley," Sisko drawled, "You're such a fun guy to hang around with. No wonder I'm always glad to see you."

O'Brien muttered something to the effect of "same to you," but Sisko was distracted by a late arrival.

"Hi!" Jadzia grinned, somewhat abashed as she

ducked through the airlock. The Trill wore her flight jacket and carried a large duffel slung over her shoulder. Her face was slightly reddened, making the spots around her forehead and down the sides of her face stand out. "Is the offer still open?"

Sisko knew this was his lucky day. "Come on in, and let's discuss it." To O'Brien, he ordered, "Power them up and make sure the replicators are working."

O'Brien glumly shuffled toward engineering as Jadzia dumped her duffel onto the flight deck. She let out her breath in relief. "Whew! I stored as much as I could. They've impounded the *Rogue Star* until I pay the rest of the docking fees."

Sisko was busy closing the airlock. He wouldn't put it past Garak to plant a listening device on his ship, but Sisko had taken the precaution of installing dampers throughout the *Denorios*. It would take a very powerful device to pierce dampers and a sealed airlock.

As the seal formed, he asked, "Your friend couldn't help you?"

"Friend!" Jadzia raised one dark brow. "She's no friend of mine. She acted like she didn't know who I was."

"I thought you worked together."

Jadzia hesitated again, obviously unwilling to talk about her business.

Smoothly, Sisko told her, "I like to know something about people I hire." As Jadzia continued to remain silent, he added, "This is a very lucrative position, with perks from working directly for the Intendant of Bajor. There are plenty of people who would like to be in your boots."

"Then why are you short one crew member?" Jadzia countered.

Sisko liked her spunk, and he certainly admired those curves, but he wanted more from this deal. He wanted to know about Seven.

"I'm picky about who I crew with." Sisko let that speak for itself.

Reluctantly, Jadzia said, "What do you want to know?"

Sisko let his satisfaction show. "Tell me what you know about Seven. Where is she from? Who does she work for?"

"I don't know much," Jadzia protested. "I've transported her three times, from this place to that."

"Why didn't she use her own shuttlecraft?"

"She didn't say." Jadzia smiled wryly. "She doesn't talk much, if you noticed."

"I noticed." Sisko chuckled, but he wasn't letting it go. "Where did you take her?"

"Last trip was from the Klingon territory to Balancar, a colony in the former Terran Empire."

"What was a Terran doing in Klingon territory?"

Jadzia shrugged. "I don't know. That was part of the transport agreement—no questions."

"Do you know where she's from?"

"That's just it! There's no telling with her."

Narrowing his eyes, Sisko knew that Jadzia was hiding something. She was looking distinctly uncomfortable.

"Why are you protecting her?" he asked. "I'm offering you a way to get your ship back. Who knows, you may like this work and decide to stay on. It's been profitable for me and my crew . . ."

Jadzia's hands twisted together. She wasn't as confident now, and Sisko could tell the Trill didn't have any good options. If she didn't have the docking fees, she also didn't have a way to pay for quarters on Terok Nor. As an indigent, she would be thrown into the brig, then into the slave compound to work off what she owed in fines and fees.

Sisko glanced at the chrono. "You're out of time. Decide whose side you're on."

They could hear the voices of his crew on the flight deck and the engineers calling to each other on the deck below. Clearly the ship was ready to depart.

"All right," she agreed. "I'll tell you, but you can't let anyone know where you got this information."

Sisko looked dubious. "Sure."

"I mean it," Jadzia insisted. "I'm scared of her. I almost didn't recognize her as a Terran, and she tried to act like she didn't know me. But I could tell she was surprised. I've never seen her look the same way twice. She's been Andorian, Benzar, Trill, and twice she was Bajoran. Whenever I met her before, we used a countersign."

"Who do you think she is?" Sisko prompted, thoroughly intrigued.

Jadzia looked both ways down the deck to be sure they weren't overheard. "I think she's Cardassian."

Sisko couldn't believe that. "Nah . . . not her."

"Yes," she insisted. "There's something creepy about her. Reminds me of Cardassians I've done business for."

Sisko doubted it was true. But he couldn't help smiling at what Kira would say if her new favorite turned out to be Cardassian. "Anything else?"

A flash of irritation shot from her eyes. "What else do you want—the keys to the Grand Nagus's vaults?"

When he continued to stare at her, Jadzia's tone became more wheedling. "Come on, I've told you everything I know. I kept my side of the bargain. If she knew, she'd probably slit my throat. You can tell from her eyes that she would do it."

Sisko let himself smile. He liked this woman. "Welcome aboard the *Denorios,* Jadzia. You do your job and you'll get an equal share of the take."

Jadzia was relieved, and obviously pleased to have struck the bargain. She shook his hand, then swung her duffel over her shoulder, heading off to find his second-in-command to report in. Meanwhile, O'Brien came shuffling back up to the flight deck, his gloomy report confirming that the replicators were now working perfectly.

Sisko clapped him on the shoulder, "Cheer up, Smiley! I'll be gone for the next couple of weeks."

"Doing the Intendant's dirty work," O'Brien agreed sourly.

"Someone has to do it," Sisko agreed. He popped the airlock and let it cycle open so O'Brien could get out.

"Yeah, well enjoy it while it lasts," O'Brien said with sudden pluck. "The Intendant might choose someone else to collect the duties for her . . . She seems to have a new favorite every week."

"That's why I like you, Smiley, because you're so simpleminded." Sisko laughed. "Kira doesn't keep good things to herself. All I have to do is wait, and I'll get mine in the end."

Sisko was still laughing at O'Brien's expression as he cycled the airlock closed behind him.

Chapter 16

AGENT SEVEN REPORTED to the transporter room on Terok Nor. She had an errand to run for Kira, taking a message disc to the Third Minister of Bajor. Several times since her arrival Kira had asked Seven to perform small tasks, testing her competence and loyalty. A few days ago, Seven had taken a load of isolinear rods to Kira's docking master on Bajor VII. She used her repaired shuttlecraft and discovered it worked better than before the crash. This time, Seven was beaming directly to Bajor from Terok Nor's high orbit around the home planet.

For the past two weeks Seven had played the part of a weary merchant pilot getting a hard-earned rest. She slept late, ate the delicious food, and swam in the long green pool. She lounged on the sofas and watched Kira. It was an odd game they played, with Kira obviously curious but fearing her as an unknown entity. They were never alone together, and there were several other people around whenever Seven saw Kira. Kira seemed intrigued by her indifferent attitude, and constantly asked for her to be present in her "inner sanctum." Seven complied while responding coolly to Kira's probing questions.

While her slaves carefully tended and entertained her, Kira acted as Overseer and Intendant, reading reports and giving orders to her staff. When she wanted privacy, she put up a baffling cone around her, a nearly invisible shield that blocked sound waves. That allowed her slaves to continue polishing her nails or rubbing her feet. Due to a distortion in the baffling cone, Seven was unable to read Kira's lips, so she affected an air of disinterest.

The arrangements changed when Worf arrived at Terok Nor. Seven's odd tentative relationship with Kira shifted, and she was moved from the cabana adjacent to the pool to private quarters in the habitat ring. Seven took the opportunity to roam the station, getting to know the layout and personnel. It was overflowing with boisterous Klingons celebrating their recent victory against the Romulans. Over and over again she heard the name Duras proclaimed as the champion of the battle. She knew the Klingons would tear her apart in an instant if they found out that she had killed Duras.

Sometimes Kira and Worf strolled together on the Promenade or through the corridors. Kira often smiled at Seven but never paused to speak. Everyone else on the station treated Seven with a mixture of distaste and respect, clearly believing she had an alliance with Kira. They feared her influence with the Intendant yet scorned her because she was Terran.

When Seven materialized in the Bajoran Chamber of Ministers, she was immediately challenged by the transporter chief because of her Terran appearance. When her orders were confirmed by Terok Nor Ops, she was given a large red tag to wear around her neck, certifying she had permission to be in the complex.

Everyone in the wide hallways either ignored her or nervously tried to avoid her. Seven kept her brown hood pulled over her hair, hating the way it drew attention. If she had known that her natural hair color would be so distinctive, she would have dyed it dark. For some reason, Enabran Tain had not thought it necessary to brief her on Terran characteristics and behavior.

Seven had not been Terran since she was six years old, and it was more unpleasant than she remembered. Even though Kira's private quarters had a cloying and loathsome ambience, Seven preferred that blessed isolation to these negative reactions. Her brain and character were Cardassian. The flesh could be altered, while the will endured.

Seven had memorized a map of the large complex, so she didn't have to ask directions to get to the Third Minister's offices. The pale gray corridors were softly lit by wall sconces that cast a warm yellow light. The ambient sound was relatively subdued, and she believed the flooring was designed both to absorb sound waves and to cushion the impact of footsteps.

A complex overlay of scents filtered through the corridors, indicating an abundance of surrounding vegetation. An open window near her destination lured her closer, so she paused and took a deep breath. She had been on starships and stations since her mission began, breathing recycled air. There was something spicy growing nearby, and it suddenly made her sneeze.

"Move along," a guard ordered.

"I have business with the Third Minister." Seven gestured toward the door across the hall.

"Then go," the guard told her brusquely. "You can't loiter here."

The guard didn't look directly at her. He swung the communications wand as he scanned the passing bureaucrats. Seven found his manner highly offensive, but she didn't want to draw attention to herself. She silently crossed the hall and entered the Third Minister's office.

Fortunately, the Third Minister was not in. Since Seven had orders from Kira to hand the message disc directly to the minister himself, Seven refused to leave it with the receptionist. Instead she insisted she would deliver it when the minister returned from his midday meal.

Now was her chance to work on her real mission—finding out who was behind the assassination plot. Seven had been patient, knowing that Kira would be carefully watching her. Any step out of character would end in failure. But now she had been handed time in the very place she needed to be. Kira was preoccupied by Worf's visit to Terok Nor. When she had given Seven the assignment, she had been rushing to prepare for a conference call later today with the major Intendants. Seven thought it unlikely that her movements would be tracked.

Seven proceeded down the corridor toward her quarry

in the First Minister's office. She was looking for the woman who had been with Leeta on Bajor XII.

Enabran Tain had prepared Seven for this mission by including in the burst transmission a database of all known individuals of Cardassian descent living in the Bajoran sector. Over the past few weeks, as Seven appeared to be lazing around Kira's pool, her cranial implant had run the unknown woman's voice against recognition patterns gathered by Obsidian Order agents. She replayed the woman's question over and over again, "How do we know you won't inform on us?" Ironic, considering that Seven had immediately informed on them.

There were tens of thousands of individuals loosely or not so loosely allied with Cardassia who were living in the Bajoran system. Seven ran a comparison on both men and women because she knew from past experience how easy it was to pose as someone of the opposite gender. Her implant placed each spiked graph directly on her retina for comparison so no one could tell what she was doing.

After many long days of comparing graphs, Seven had finally located a voice match for the woman with the shadowed face. Her name was Tora Ziyal, a cherished assistant to the First Minister of Bajor, Winn Adami. Ziyal's heritage was noted as Bajoran and Cardassian.

Seven would not allow herself to speculate on who was behind the assassination plot until she had confirmed the voice correlation with Ziyal.

The reception room of the First Minister was luxurious in a way that startled Seven's senses. Everything was made of natural material: polished wood, fine-grained marble, and smooth fur upholstery. The reception desk was inlaid with chips of ivory, coral, and mother-of-pearl, forming an abstract swirling pattern that flowed down onto the floor. One wall supported holo-images of Winn Adami at various ceremonies and events.

A young Bajoran man was keying in something at the computer terminal. In a faintly disapproving tone, he asked, "May I help you?"

"Yes," Seven said, approaching the desk. "I would like to see Tora Ziyal."

"Yes, well, I'm sure she's very busy." The receptionist didn't pause, tapping out a rapid code on his terminal. "What is this in reference to?"

Seven had an irrational urge to strike out at these people and force them to take her seriously. It ran counter to her training, so she sternly repressed the impulse.

She lifted the message disc from her waist pouch, letting it shift so only the receptionist—and not the overhead cameras—could see the insignia of Terok Nor. It was addressed to the Third Minister, but the receptionist couldn't tell that.

"Right . . ." The receptionist was clearly taken aback. "I'll get Tora Ziyal." He adjusted the stem of his earpiece. "You may wait over there."

The receptionist murmured a few quick words to summon the assistant. Seven positioned herself where she could see the archway he kept glancing at. She was certain she could talk her way out of this if Tora Ziyal was not the woman who had been in the bar on Bajor XII.

But when Ziyal appeared, Seven knew that she had

found the right one. Ziyal broke stride, her mouth open
ing slightly in recognition.

Seven instantly noted her Cardassian features, though
they were blurred and softened, along with the distinctive Bajoran nose wrinkle. Ziyal was quite young, and
her slender frame seemed weighed down by the ma-
genta robes of office that indicated she was part of the
ministerial class. A rust-colored skullcap concealed her
hair, while the overdrape was caught up on the left side
of her chest with a large silver ring.

Seven smoothly moved forward to cover Ziyal's confusion. "I have a message."

Ziyal hesitated, glancing at the receptionist, who
quickly pretended to be busy with his work. Seven met
Ziyal's eyes with unwavering intent.

"Certainly, this way," Ziyal murmured.

Following Ziyal through the maze of rooms—mostly
storage closets and hallways—Seven got the impression
she was being taken the back way in order to avoid prying eyes. That suited her fine.

Ziyal was acting increasingly nervous, no doubt as
she considered the danger of being seen with Seven. She
kept looking around to make sure no one was watching
before hurrying through the hallways. Seven pulled her
hood farther over her face.

As Ziyal ushered her into a small room, she whispered, "What are you doing here?"

"Is there any possibility we are being monitored?"
Seven had to ask. Ziyal seemed green enough to do almost anything, like have a discussion about assassinating the Overseer underneath a security camera.

"No, we do an EM sweep every day to make sure nothing's been planted," Ziyal assured her.

Seven quickly assessed the spare furnishings. A computer station was made of dark polished wood and the panels on four walls hid office equipment. The chairs had wooden frames with green cloth cushions, but Seven chose to stand near the door. She didn't like being in rooms that had only one exit.

"What about your own people?" Seven wanted to be sure no one would pick up the recording she was ready to make. "Don't they monitor what goes on in here?"

"This is my private office." Ziyal's eyes were wide. "First Minister Winn would never allow that."

"I see," Seven said noncommittally. Whether Ziyal was remarkably naive or it was true that no one was keeping an eye on the staff, Seven activated her implant to begin recording. "I have encountered a problem, and you are the one I could contact without raising suspicions."

"You were supposed to contact Leeta, not me." Ziyal glanced at her computer, no doubt wishing she could call Leeta and let her know. "How did you know who I was?"

Seven would not be distracted. "I will cancel the contract unless this problem is resolved."

"What's wrong?" Ziyal took a few steps closer. "Leeta told me you're living with Kira on the station. Why don't you go ahead and . . . do it?" Her delicate face showed her distaste at the nature of the job.

"Kira distrusts everyone, including her slaves." Seven lifted her chin slightly. "The security is so tight that I will not be able to get out alive. I will be caught and interrogated. After that Cardassian security chief extracts the information from me, you and Leeta will be implicated."

"Oh . . ." Ziyal seemed frightened. "When Leeta told me . . . I thought everything was settled. Isn't there some way you can escape?"

"There is one way." Seven held her gaze. "I will have to surrender, and no doubt I will be tortured. Someone with enough influence will have to get me released into their custody before I break."

"You mean . . ." Ziyal drew back. "You want me to get the First Minister involved in this? Oh, no. I can't do that—"

Seven took two steps forward, leaning down right into the startled girl's face. "She *must* get involved if she wants the job done."

Ziyal's mouth opened, but nothing came out.

Seven pressed her advantage. "Besides, I have doubts Winn Adami could get custody of me. Winn may be First on Bajor, but she is nothing to the Alliance. That Cardassian security chief on Terok Nor may take precedence."

"Oh, no, Winn will have plenty of influence over Terok Nor," Ziyal quickly assured her. "She's perfectly placed to take over the Intendant's position."

"How do you know?" Seven retorted. "The Alliance will choose the next Intendant, not the Bajorans."

"I have it on good authority that Winn Adami will be named Intendant if something happens to Kira."

Seven knew she was onto something. "Whose authority?" When Ziyal stayed silent, she insisted, "You are only Winn's Third Assistant. I trust my judgment more than yours. And you should, too. That's why you hired a professional. I must have the information in order to complete this job."

Ziyal made a move toward the computer. "Maybe I should call Leeta—"

Seven caught her arm through the full sleeve. "Tell me now. Every second I am here, we are all at risk. Including the First Minister."

Ziyal tensed. "Just do it. I'm sure Winn will be able to take control of Terok Nor quickly. Things are already being done to ease her way into the Intendant's position . . ."

"By who?" Seven held her breath.

"Deanna Troi, the Intendant of Betazed." Ziyal added in a rush, "She's the Regent's companion, so you know she'll be able to get whatever she wants. He'll assign Winn as temporary Intendant."

Seven released Ziyal's arm, smoothing down her robe. It was astonishing how simple some people were. "Does Leeta know about this?"

"Yes. Leeta is completely loyal to Winn." Ziyal seemed worried, yet she was clearly proud of her superior. "This will be so good for our people, something we've needed for a long time. We can't wait any longer."

"Yes," Seven agreed. "I can complete the contract under the original terms."

Ziyal sighed in relief. "We have to know the moment . . . it happens. You won't suffer too much, will you?"

"I'm sure I will survive," Seven said dryly.

"After all, it is for the good of Bajorans everywhere," Ziyal reminded her.

* * *

As Seven returned to the mellow halls of the Ministry complex to complete her delivery for Kira, she replayed the conversation she had just had with Ziyal. No matter how innocent people seemed, deep down, everyone was basically alike—selfish and self-righteous. The thought made Seven feel empty and hopeless, though she wasn't sure why.

Chapter 17

DEEP IN THE bunkers of the Obsidian Order, in his round command room, Enabran Tain received a case that had just been delivered. The code on the lock indicated it held Garak's report, conveyed from Terok Nor by personal courier. The report was a week early.

Inside the foam-lined case were several message rods and one-half of a small silver sphere. An emergency communications beacon. Agents sent a beacon when they needed direct audio consultation with Tain, most often to report mission failure and request an emergency pullout.

The Order had lost track of several agents during the recent Klingon offensive against the Romulans. The Klingons had taken several sectors from the Romulans along the Alpha Quadrant border. Regent Worf had led the "glorious" offensive in the name of Duras. In Tain's opinion, it had been a tactical error, a waste of starships and munitions to gain systems that were of dubious value to the Alliance.

The Cardassians had not participated, but several agents had been swept into the battle and had not made contact since. Tain hoped the message was from one of his missing agents. He wanted real data on the damage that had been inflicted, not vague exaggerations from the Klingons.

Tain dropped the beacon into the fission unit to split the trithium from the electromagnetic signal. Meanwhile, he activated Garak's report. After the first few inconsequential words, Tain hardly listened to Garak's drawling remarks about the situation on Terok Nor. Mostly he continued monitoring the data streams projected on various screens and readouts that encircled the small command room.

It was annoying the way Garak said one thing while his tone said another. Agents should be forthright and succinct. It was incomprehensible to Tain how that boy's mother could have borne such a mealymouthed weakling. His former wife had been a woman of few words until the day she left the bunker forever. Then he had never heard from her again.

Garak was saying with a smirk, *"As for your other little project, I've lent her an emergency beacon and thought you'd like to receive it immediately."* Obviously pleased with himself, he added, *"I'm sure you'll agree that I made the right decision . . ."*

"Pompous idiot," Tain muttered under his breath. So the communications beacon was from Agent Seven. But he doubted it was a pullout. It was true that Seven had failed to accomplish her missions several times before, but she had always extracted herself and left the situation prepared for the arrival of another agent.

"I have been observing the situation," Garak continued. *"She has been doing exactly as I suggested to intrigue . . . our friend. I'm glad to see you've put my reports to good use. If you would like, I could offer a more detailed report on the characteristics of 'our friend' which I believe could be exploited . . ."*

The fission unit beeped, indicating the signal had been extracted and a secured audio channel was open in subspace. The only sound was a faint hissing of the open channel, waiting for the other half of the beacon to be activated. Sometimes the beacon was never activated and the agent was never heard from again. In the past, Tain had left the unit functioning and the channel open for days, giving his agents plenty of time to open their end of the link. He was prepared to stay in his command room until Agent Seven answered.

". . . and in my unique position," Garak was saying, trying to look modest. *"I believe I am best placed to perform this duty—"*

Tain abruptly clicked off the report. Garak's voice only served to irritate him. If there was anything of importance, the computer would tag it as it analyzed the standard reports from the thousands of Obsidian Order agents planted across the galaxy.

An indicator light on his desk panel glowed red, a signal from the guards at the surface entrance to the bunker. "What is it?" Tain asked tersely.

"Sir, Gul Dukat is here," the guard reported. "He says he must see you."

Tain switched on the viewscreen to see Gul Dukat's broad shoulders filling the entryway to the turbolift. His neck ridges were distended wider than his scowling face. One hand was clenched into a fist, and he held his wrist tightly as if restraining himself. Dukat told the guard flatly, *"Tain has no choice. He will see me."*

So, the day of reckoning was finally at hand. "Let him down," Tain ordered.

He had been waiting for this development, though he hadn't expected Dukat to visit the hidden bunker. Gul Dukat had been rapidly gaining power in Cardassia since his nearly successful bid for Overseer. Because he had lost by only one vote, the Cardassians viewed him as the unofficial heir apparent to the Overseer's position. Dukat was considered to be a galactic force, able to command the respect of entire empires.

As a consequence, Dukat had increased his efforts to investigate his father's trial and execution. He needed to vindicate his father to remove the last bit of tarnish from his own name.

Tain assumed it was only a matter of time before Dukat would discover something that led to Garak. Tain couldn't trust Garak's competence. He must have made some mistakes in planting the evidence against Dukat's father. But Tain had been forced to use Garak because he would do anything, even things that other agents might question.

Gul Dukat stepped into the small command room, glaring down at Tain over the banks of monitors. Tain rested his hands on the curved desk, his finger on the "dead man's key" that would summon his guards if released.

Dukat narrowed his eyes, moving stiffly as he began to circle the desk. "I wanted to tell you myself."

Tain didn't move, even as Dukat came closer to the wraparound terminal.

"I knew it was you," Dukat whispered. "But now I know how you did it. You used your own son." Dukat leaned forward. "You made it personal. So now I'm making it personal."

"Your threats are inconsequential," Tain shot back. His finger remained on the translucent square.

"I intend to tell the Cardassian Union how you framed my father. I'll call for your resignation!"

Tain didn't blink in the face of Dukat's rage. His voice was deceptively calm. "You do not have the necessary votes on the Detapa Council to remove me from the Obsidian Order."

"No?" Dukat put his fists on top of the monitors on Tain's desk. "I think you are mistaken, old man."

Tain smiled slightly. "You're not that stupid, Dukat. It will split the Council, and without the support of a united Cardassian Union, you will never become Overseer."

Suddenly the emergency beacon beeped in the fission unit, indicating the channel had been opened from the other side. Tain immediately lifted his finger, and Obsidian security poured into the command room.

"I have work to do," Tain told Dukat, "to ensure Cardassia's place in the Alliance. I had assumed that was your goal as well." To the guards, he said, "Escort Gul Dukat to the surface."

Dukat held firm by the desk, sneering at Tain. "Every breath you take is by my grace. You will pay for what you have done!"

At a nod from Tain, the senior guard intervened between them, urging Dukat to step away from the desk. With one last glare over his shoulder, Dukat shook off their hands and stalked from the room. The guards quickly followed, avoiding Tain's gaze.

Tain didn't know if Dukat would announce his findings publicly or whether he would covertly attempt to generate sentiment against him. If he was smart, he would do the latter. Regardless, Tain would have to prepare contingency responses.

Tain waited only a moment after the turbolift closed and took Gul Dukat back to the surface. He wouldn't allow Dukat to disrupt his concentration for any longer than that. Then he activated the communications beacon, accessing the direct subspace channel between his location and Agent Seven on Terok Nor. This technology had also been developed by his research scientists, and was secure to within a .004 percent margin of error.

"Report," Tain ordered.

The channel could carry only sound waves, so there was no image. As usual, to gather as much information as possible, Tain activated the emotigraph. The emotigraph computer program provided a constant analysis and readout of the emotional state and conviction rate of the agent when compared to their bio-norms.

Seven's voice came through clear and crisp. *"First Minister Winn Adami of Bajor is responsible for the contract on Kira Nerys. Her assistant, Tora Ziyal, was the woman with Leeta on Bajor Twelve. Tora Ziyal reports that Deanna Troi, Intendant of Betazed, will back Winn's bid to become the next Intendant of Bajor."*

With a minimum of words, Seven described her meeting with the half-Bajoran, half-Cardassian Ziyal. Tain silently approved of the way she had recorded the conversation. However, as Seven spoke about her success in gaining proximity to Kira among the slaves, the emotigraph indicated a rise in her anxiety level.

"It would be possible to complete the contract as specified," Seven concluded. *"What are my orders?"*

Tain was intrigued by Deanna Troi's involvement in this. This meant the Klingons could ultimately be responsible for the assassination attempt. Not that Klingons would officially approve of assassination. But Troi might take it upon herself if it was in their best interests to dispose of Kira.

That was a moot point, however. Kira must remain Overseer while Dukat's power was growing. If Dukat became Overseer now, he would be able to force Tain to retire from the Obsidian Order.

Tain could not allow Kira to be assassinated. "I don't want Kira harmed. Instead, tell her that Winn hired you to assassinate her. Make sure the accomplices are interrogated to confirm Troi's involvement."

"Understood," Seven said shortly.

Tain kept a close eye on the emotigraph. He wished he could see Seven's expression. He could sense that something was wrong, but he couldn't pinpoint what it was.

"Stay by Kira's side," Tain ordered. "Get closer to

her. Make her trust you. Tell her that she has seduced you, and that's why you're betraying Winn."

There was a slight pause. *"Kira will be suspicious. She trusts no one."*

The emotigraph again shifted on the fight-or-flight level. There was a basic conflict within Seven, yet Tain was convinced that her training would overcome any qualms she might have about encouraging such a dangerous liaison. Kira's behavior was known to be extreme, but Seven could handle it.

"I'm sure you've thoroughly analyzed the situation. There must be a way you can prove your sincerity."

"Perhaps . . ." Seven started, then trailed off.

Tain noted her hesitation. "Perhaps you can offer to kill Winn in retaliation."

"Understood," Seven replied, causing another minor tremor on the emotigraph.

"Good. Garak will keep me appraised. Tain out." It wasn't perfect, but at least it would keep Winn from making another attempt on Kira's life and give him time to deal with Dukat.

Enabran Tain spent the rest of the night poring over background data on those involved in the assassination plot against Kira. Winn Adami's motive was clear. She had been a beloved disciple of Intendant Opaka and was undoubtedly balancing the score with Kira. However, Deanna Troi's motives would require extensive investigation and analysis.

Tain could find nothing of interest in the background of the Bajoran, Leeta. She was from the Shakaar province and had worked in the Central Archives for nearly a decade. Otherwise she was a typical malcontent with a history of political activism who had somehow met up with Winn Adami.

Ziyal, on the other hand, turned out to be quite intriguing. She had been orphaned while a young child, and Tain could not identify her Cardassian father. Oddly enough, it was not part of public or family court record.

Tain ran his Bajoran administrative files through his standard seeker program, which carefully correlated each bit of information and association that was uncovered. This complex program delved not only into the subjects' past, but that of their family, friends, and coworkers as well.

Tain had infinite patience for this sort of work. He certainly wasn't expecting the program to sound a priority one signal. His class-1 priority list was short, and it included people and things that were of prime importance to him. These things were automatically checked whenever a standard search was run.

This time the seeker program had found a connection to Gul Dukat. The link was deep in the records of Ziyal's mother, Tora Naprem. Naprem had been assigned to a supervisory position at the Jerom Beta mining camp ten months prior to the birth of her half-breed daughter. At the same time, Gul Dukat was the Alliance inspector of Terran slave camps, including those in Bajoran territory. He would have undoubtedly come in contact with Ziyal's mother.

Checking quickly, Tain discovered there were not many Cardassians on Jerom Beta at the time, and only three were male. It was a simple procedure to access their medical records and DNA signatures. Likely one of these men was Ziyal's father, but he would leave no possibility unexamined, especially when it concerned Gul Dukat.

Tain assigned an agent to go immediately to Bajor to get a tissue sample from Ziyal. Only her genes could tell him what he needed to know.

Chapter 18

KIRA WAS BORED now that Worf had left again, and she was using her padd to flip through the remote viewing channels of various areas on Terok Nor. Then she saw Seven signing for a large container in cargo bay 16. Seven carried it in one hand by the middle strap, holding the tubular container horizontal to the ground. Kira clicked from one channel to the next, following her via the screen on her padd as Seven made her way through the access tube from the docking ring.

Kira expected Seven to turn into the habitat ring toward her temporary quarters, where she had been installed during Worf's most recent visit. Kira had been looking for Seven's devious side since she had found her on Jeraddo. The Free-Terran was certainly one of the most guarded people Kira had ever encountered, rarely laughing and almost never making small talk

Seven hadn't attempted to ingratiate herself with Kira in any way. Kira found that refreshing.

Seven continued through the access tube to the central core of the station, toward Kira's private quarters. After Worf left, Kira had ordered Seven to move her things back to one of the cabanas next to the pool. She assumed Seven would take her mysterious package there.

Kira signaled her majordomo. "Serge, please do a level-1 scan on the container Seven is bringing in. Tell her it's standard procedure. I want to know what's inside down to the last atom."

An hour later, while Kira was getting a massage from her favorite slave, her majordomo signaled that the scan was complete. She lazily tapped the sequence that would lower the baffler so she wouldn't have to tell Marani to stop.

"Overseer," the majordomo reported, *"the container holds a rudimentary holo-imager. We could find no additional components or devices within the imager."*

"Really . . ." Kira murmured thoughtfully. "Give it back to Seven, then."

Tapping the baffler away, Kira sighed. "You have the best hands, Marani."

It wasn't long before Seven appeared, carrying the large black container. She went to a gold ottoman on the other side of the pool chamber and set the container on end next to her. The bulky cylinder towered over her head. It was an intriguing thing, but Kira preferred to complete her massage rather than question her now. She liked to test the people around her, but as usual, Seven was the embodiment of patience.

Finally, Kira could contain her curiosity no longer. It was a pleasant feeling, rather rare these days. She had been concentrating on her Overseer duties, making momentous decisions that affected the lives of billions of sentient creatures. Much-needed revenue was pouring into Bajoran markets, and the quotas on "volunteers" for the front had been shifted to ease the burden on her own people. Everyone was prosperous and happy, except for the other Intendants. But she didn't mind that. They would appreciate it more when she eased up on them.

But the Overseer's duties were complex and took so much of her time that she had little time left for amusement in her life. Even Worf had not been swayed by her charms during his last visit, despite the drinking and celebration that went along with a victorious battle. She was beginning to realize that his emotional bond with the Betazoid was stronger than she had anticipated. She was already working on ways to break down his resistance, but Worf's visits were too few and far between for her to make any headway. Something would have to be done about that soon.

"Thank you, Marani," Kira said, swinging her legs over the side of the padded lounge. She always believed in being polite to her slaves. Anyone who touched her body was worthy of respect.

"Why, Seven . . . what's in the container?" Kira drawled in pretend surprise. "Are you leaving us? I thought your delivery date wasn't until next week."

Seven brought the container closer. "I would like to give you something."

"A present? For me?" Kira was vaguely disappointed. People who gave gifts always expected something in return. "What is it?"

Seven seemed uncomfortable. "I would rather show you in private."

Kira hesitated, looking into Seven's remarkably steady eyes. The cleft in her chin was enchanting, and for that reason alone, Kira agreed. She tapped out an alert for her majordomo, knowing security would be waiting at every door. Then she clapped her hands and waved for the other slaves to depart.

When the last door slid closed, Kira smiled at Seven. "You have my complete attention."

Seven opened the top of the container, revealing sets of gauges and a computer panel. Kira felt her heart speed up, an instinctive reaction to the unknown. Not an entirely unpleasant feeling, especially because her people would have detected anything that was dangerous.

"This is a portable holo-imager," Seven explained. "It cannot create people or complex environments, but it can do this."

Suddenly walls materialized close around them, shiny gold with curved fitted joints. Kira knew the holo-imager was creating the illusion, but the effect was startling.

"It's a spaceship," Kira said.

"A Bajoran solar-sail," Seven agreed.

Kira deliberately went to the wall and touched the cold metal. Through the portal she could see the stars and their slight movement, indicating they were in motion.

"We're still in my quarters?" Kira had to ask.

"Yes, I can turn off the image if you—"

"No," Kira interrupted. She didn't want to destroy the illusion. For a moment, she liked wondering if she was on a real lightship. Maybe Seven had kidnapped her.

Looking up, the top portal revealed the tips of the great curving sails, shining ruddy in the light of Bajor. She could even feel the slight rocking that came from the tenuous solar wind.

Kira's legs were braced apart, and her eyes briefly closing as Seven cranked down the sails and changed their course. "This is perfect," she finally said.

"I thought you would like it," Seven replied softly. She was standing at the navigation rings. "You said you hadn't been able to get away and relax. I remembered you had said something about your family having a solar-sail when you were young."

"Yes." Kira could hardly remember that golden time before her family had been broken apart forever. She had been a child, a different person back then. But her body remembered the feel of the lightship, and Seven's careful adjustments of the navigation rings reminded her of her mother's slender hands performing the same task. She preferred to remember her mother as she was then, rather than later, when she had lived with Dukat.

Kira circled the ship, feeling a sense of recognition at the fittings and cramped quarters. Finally she sat on the curved bench, leaning back against the wall and looking up at Seven. Kira knew that this was not by chance.

Seven had put too much thought and effort into finding exactly the right gift.

"You've surprised me, Seven, and that isn't easy to do."

"I'm glad," Seven said simply. Her feet were spread apart to ride the subtle shifts in the vessel. "I'm not good at expressing my feelings. I wanted to give you something to show you how much I care about you."

"Why, Seven! I'm touched." Kira waited, wanting to hear more.

Seven's chin rose. "There is no other explanation for what I must tell you." Her hands were clasped behind her, almost as if she were standing at attention. "Your life is in danger."

Kira sat up straighter. "In general, or do you mean specifically?"

Seven finally met her eyes. "I was hired by Winn Adami . . . to assassinate you."

"What!" Kira leaped to her feet.

Seven held out her hand as if to reassure her. "I could not do it. I knew from the first day I saw you. But the First Minister is determined. Next time her people will hire a professional. Perhaps they already have."

"Prove it," Kira demanded. She was back to wondering if she really was on a lightship. She felt confused and exhilarated at the same time.

"I have a recording of my meeting with Winn's Third Assistant." Seven handed over the tiny disc. "I couldn't tell you until I had proof that Winn was involved."

Kira thought fast. "Why are you telling me now? Why not leave if you changed your mind? I could throw you into the slave compound for this."

"I know, but I had to warn you." Seven jerked her chin again. "I am worried about you. Winn is not the only one behind the assassination plot."

"No?" Kira sat down again. "There's more?"

Seven nodded seriously. "Deanna Troi has assured Winn that she will be made Intendant of Bajor if you are killed." She gestured to the disc Kira had taken. "That is what the Third Assistant says."

Kira considered the tiny disc. "The Intendant of Betazed . . . Anyone else? The Cardassians? The Klingons? I'm sure there are plenty of people who would be thrilled to see me dead and gone."

Seven shook her head. "That's everything I know. I am sorry, I wish to make amends to you."

"Why?" Kira wondered if the plot was Troi's whim to have her removed, or if this revealed something deeper. Did Worf know about the assassination contract? That was the real question. Did Troi want her killed because she was a threat, or was Worf playing her for a fool?

"I told you because . . ." Seven faltered. "I have never met anyone like you. You are more alive than other people."

Kira felt touched in spite of herself. Here she was considering great galactic machinations, and this sweet girl was confessing her love. She liked Terrans just as she liked all of her fine possessions. She liked so-called Free-Terrans even better because they offered a challenge. Most of them took pride in not belonging to anyone. She enjoyed proving them wrong, then keeping them around in devoted servitude. As long as they entertained her.

This one was certainly more entertaining than most.

Perhaps she would be useful, as well. "Why should I trust you?"

"I will prove my loyalty to you. I will do anything you ask."

Kira raised one brow, stepping closer. "Anything?" she asked teasingly.

Seven swallowed, saying low, *"That* is my fondest desire."

Kira was impressed by the raw emotion in Seven's voice. She had never seen Seven like this. But then it was only a natural reaction after joining her intimate circle . . . and reminded of that, Kira knew someone would have to pay for their mistake. Why hadn't the security checks discovered Seven's past associations?

"First Minister Winn . . ." Kira said through clenched teeth. "Something will have to be done about her."

"Let me do it." Seven went to her knees in front of Kira, her fingers hesitating to touch the toes of her shining boots. "I will eliminate her for you. I will do anything you ask." Her face turned up.

Kira was enchanted by Seven's declaration. "You continue to amaze me, my dear."

Her hand caressed Seven's fine hair, stroking it away from her face. There was something different about Terrans, something primitive at heart, as if they never fully developed as individuals. But in their childlike way, they were thoroughly delightful. Kira bent down to kiss Seven's forehead, savoring the thought of what she was going to do with this proud creature.

"I will let you prove your loyalty," Kira murmured, looking into her trusting eyes. "Now you belong to me."

Chapter 19

FOR THE NEXT few days, Seven walked a narrow line with Intendant Kira. She was clearly not trusted and was not allowed to leave the pool area. After their encounter in the holographic lightship, Kira was never alone with her, probably not willing to risk a change of heart.

Seven tried to relax, knowing it was inevitable that her motives would be suspect. She had been thoroughly trained in how to submerge herself in an identity, and she kept faithfully making the effort. But since the identity was really her own, and she was using her real face and being called by her code name, she felt disconcerted.

Seven had been apprehensive when she received this assignment, but being near Kira was exciting. At first she wondered if it was Kira's zest for pleasure that was infectious. But after Seven spoke with Tain via the emergency beacon, she realized she was fascinated by Kira's total autonomy. Kira was everything Seven wa not. She was self-indulgent, boisterous, and callous about getting what she wanted.

So instead of sinking into her assigned role with ease, something inside of Seven resisted. It wasn't as if she had never posed as a slave before. Early in her career, she had served undercover for half a standard year as an Orion animal woman. She had been subjected to things that Kira probably couldn't imagine. . . . Then again, maybe Kira was just taking her time. Yet Seven had never felt so personally disturbed as she did now.

Meanwhile, Kira was analyzing the copy of the recording Seven had made of her discussion with Ziyal to determine its authenticity. Seven also knew Kira was delving into her background, but she trusted Tain to bolster her cover story. One of the other slaves had mentioned the disappearance of the head of Kira's personal security operations, and an older Bajoran woman had taken his place.

When Kira finally appeared in the doorway to the pool chamber, scanning the slaves lounging on the rose-and-gold sofas, Seven knew the waiting was over.

"Are you ready to prove your loyalty to me?" Kira demanded.

Seven stood up. "Yes."

"Then come with me." Kira left the pool chamber and headed for the dressing room, forcing Seven to run after her to catch up. The other slaves followed.

Kira ordered the slaves to dress Seven in Bajoran ministerial robes. From the rust color of the overdrape, Seven knew she was supposed to be a top-level assistant. The slaves concealed her hair beneath a russet skullcap that exposed her ears. Kira gestured to Marani to fetch her box of earrings, then sifted through them with a secret smile on her face.

"Here," Kira said, holding out a chain and clasp earring to Marani. "Put this on her. She can be from the Navot territory."

Seven allowed the slaves to fasten the earring. Then they applied a wrinkled nose bridge to her face. Seven wasn't used to prosthetics, and she couldn't help twitching her nose and furrowing her brow at the cumbersome thing resting between her eyes. Surgery was more efficient.

"You can go now," Kira ordered the slaves. As Marani tucked the jewel box away, her eyes slid toward Seven with an amused smirk. Seven realized they thought Kira was dressing her up for a pleasure game.

As if to confirm everyone's suspicions, Kira led Seven to the inner sanctum. There were several scented candles lit around the bed, which stretched nearly from wall to wall in the spacious chamber.

Kira came closer to circle her. "You make a lovely Bajoran, my dear."

"Thank you." Seven waited, sensing there was more to this than casual role-play.

Kira turned to the computer desk and picked up a Klingon *taj*. "I want you to kill Winn Adami with this."

The *taj* was a Klingon knife. Instantly Seven assessed the most likely reason for using it. Doing so would put pressure on the Klingons and therefore help Kira to determine whether they were backing the assassination attempt against her. It would also benefit Kira to raise Bajoran suspicions against the Klingons, and therefore the entire Alliance. After Winn's death, Kira would un doubtedly make some fine speech about protecting their homeland against "outside galactic forces."

But that was immaterial to her primary mission. "Where?" Seven asked.

Kira rolled her eyes. "Do it in some ghastly Klingon way, in the heart, I suppose. I've heard they don't knife anyone in the back. But I have my doubts about that one."

Seven maintained her composure. "I meant, where would you like it done? How can I get close to the First Minister?"

"You're the assassin," Kira countered. "Why don't you tell me?"

Seven shook her head, reading the danger signals in Kira's voice. "I am a transport pilot, not an assassin. I accepted the contract because they offered me a fortune. You do not understand what it is like to be alone."

Hearing the real sound of distress in her voice, Seven wondered if she had said too much. But slowly, Kira began to smile. "At least an assassin wasn't hired to kill *you*."

Seven let out her breath. "I am sorry. I will do whatever you say."

Kira considered her for a moment, resting her hand on a round blue case on the desk. "You're in luck, Seven. I can get you inside the Ministry complex. An unmarked flyer will be waiting in the first slot on the south quad of the complex. All you have to do is go to the main corridor, outside the First Minister's chambers, and at the end is an entrance. You'll see the green flyer from that door."

Infiltration was usually the most important aspect of any mission. "How will I get inside?"

Kira opened the case to reveal a round metal device, roughly 30 centimeters in diameter. Seven instantly noted the wedge-and-circle symbol on the exterior and recorded it in her implant database. She strained to see the interior as Kira opened it.

"Take the *taj* in your hand," Kira ordered. "I've taken care of everything."

Seven picked up the knife as Kira faced her. Kira supported the bottom of the clamshell device so Seven could see into the top half. Her own face was reflected as Bajoran. The relief she felt at seeing herself no longer Terran made her relax somewhat.

"You've seen Winn Adami before," Kira said.

"In holo-images," Seven agreed. "Never in person."

"Don't look at me," Kira admonished. "Look into the mirror and think about Winn Adami, the way she speaks and gestures. Imagine seeing her in the mirror instead of your own face . . ."

Seven resisted the idea, but she knew that her undercover identity would do whatever Kira asked. But she felt uneasy.

"Winn Adami," Kira urged. "Think of her."

Seven used her implant database to call up one of Winn's recent speeches to her fellow Bajorans and replay the monologue. As she continued staring at the mirror, it slowly began to cloud, obscuring her own face. Then she saw Winn Adami.

"First Minister Winn—" Kira was saying.

"I see her," Seven interrupted. "The First Minister is sitting at her desk. Her hands are at her temples . . ."

"Yes!" Kira exclaimed, urging her on. "Keep on looking."

Seven examined the older woman's face, noting the lines of weariness that were etched around her mouth and eyes. Winn looked like someone who wanted desperately to lie down and sleep, but she was pushing herself to work on.

Suddenly Seven felt herself being drawn forward. She tried to resist, but there was nothing for her to hold on to. All she could see was Winn swooping closer. With a sudden jerk, she felt as if she had toppled off an invisible edge and was falling.

Seven landed on her hands and knees. Her head was reeling as she scrabbled against the slippery glazed tile.

Finally getting purchase, she leaped to her feet, holding the Klingon knife ready. The First Minister was two meters away from her, just raising her head in surprise.

Shocked, Seven couldn't help but hesitate. That wasn't a transporter. It felt like she had slid through something rather than materialized. And how did she get past the extensive security systems of the Bajoran Ministry complex?

Shaking off her confusion, Seven remembered her mission, locked on to her target, and made her move. She leaped over the desk, raising the *taj* for a fatal thrust.

Winn Adami sat quite still with an expression of uncanny calm. If she had cried out "No!" or made a defensive gesture, Seven would have done the deed and made her escape. But Winn hardly seemed surprised that a woman could drop out of nowhere, brandishing a huge blade.

Winn looked her right in the eyes. "You don't want to do this. I can tell. "

Struck by her tone, Seven couldn't help retorting, "You know nothing about me!"

Winn seemed even more weary in person. Her eyes were dim and watery, as if she had spent the night reading the business of government.

"I once was like you," Winn told Seven, ignoring the raised knife. "I was at odds with everything around me. I, too, chose to serve a higher authority." Winn leaned forward. "Then I realized there is no higher authority than my fellow people. Unless all are raised up, none are raised up. If one is trampled, we all suffer. You know what it is like to suffer alone."

"Yes," Seven whispered.

"Then cast aside your fears," Winn urged. "I can help you make your life anew. You can dedicate yourself to helping others. The one you serve now is not worthy of you."

Seven realized she was thinking about Enabran Tain. She didn't serve Kira, she served Tain. But how could she question whether Tain was worthy of her devotion? He was the only one who understood her. He was the only one who trusted and respected her.

"You're being used, my child," Winn said softly. "Only a monster could force a woman like you to kill. I can help you. I'll show you what you can become—"

Seven couldn't stand it any longer, listening in spite

of herself, hating herself for betraying Tain by her hesitation. She struck out, trying to silence Winn.

Winn surprised her by expertly parrying her thrust, knocking the knife from Seven's hand. As it skittered over the terra-cotta tile, Seven twisted away from Winn. She panicked, thinking Winn would get away, so she did the easiest thing—she broke Winn's neck.

It was terrible, and it happened too fast for her to stop and think. As Winn slumped, Seven was overwhelmed by a sense of wrong.

"No!" Seven exclaimed, bending as she eased Winn 'own and tried to soften her fall. "No, I didn't mean to . . ."

Her loss of control was complete. She didn't know what to do, how to act, or what to think. She could only stare at Winn Adami, wondering why the Bajoran's words had made sense. Seven was being used . . .

Then she remembered the flyer waiting for her outside. She had completed her mission. Why did it feel like her chest was being compressed, as if she was slowly being suffocated?

Seven stood up and backed away, wishing she was anywhere but here. With her hands trembling, she managed to slip out of Winn's chamber unseen.

Seven hurried through the hallways instinctively following the same route that Ziyal had shown her because here was no surveillance in the back areas. Seven couldn't stop thinking she was going to run into Ziyal, and she kept looking for the young woman.

The intruder alert didn't sound until Seven was near

the side entrance to the complex. There was so much
confusion in those first few seconds that she was able to
slip outside. No wonder Kira hadn't been worried about
her escape. It was Seven's experience that most public
buildings were designed to keep people from getting in
rather than monitoring those who left. But how did that
device get her inside the complex undetected? The en
tire thing felt like a hallucination.

Dazed by the brilliant sun, Seven quickly found the
parking quad. But before the guards had spread out to
cover the grounds, she reached the green flyer with it
jaunty space wings and slid through the open hatch.

"Need a ride?" the pilot drawled.

Seven recognized the Free-Terran who worked for
Kira, the man they called Sisko. He always seemed to be
leering at something. Now he was leering at her. She
had met him once before in Kira's quarters, and had had
to forcibly remove his hands from her person.

"It would be wise to leave," she told him. "The alarm
has been raised."

"At your service," Sisko replied, engaging engines
They lifted with a wobble and started to turn. "I can't
wait to get back to Terok Nor."

"Why?" Seven asked, still feeling disoriented.

Sisko licked his lips, looking at her sideways. "Kira
always gives me a cut of the cargo."

Seven clenched her teeth, wanting to cover her ears to
shut out the sound of his laughter. He clearly thought it
was a good joke. He didn't know how lucky he was that
she had left the knife behind.

Chapter 20

LEETA WAS SEATED at her terminal in the Bajoran Central Archives when she heard the first cries. Her post was tucked away in a maze of computer banks and terminals, linking the knowledge of Bajor with businesses, learning centers, and government agencies across their territory. But the word spread quickly. First Minister Winn Adami had been killed.

The archivists gathered in the junctions of the narrow corridors, shocked and denying the possibility. "Klingons!" was the outraged cry. Yet their tears and wringing hands made it clear they accepted the unbelievable. They were already mourning their beloved leader.

Leeta used the commotion to get to the service tube, avoiding the platform to the lifts that was jammed with wailing archivists. Going up eight stories in the tube, she reached the hatchway to the upper parking tiers.

In the safety of her ground flyer, her shaking hands

opened her communicator. The direct link to her cell leader was busy. Leeta would have to wait until she was contacted with her orders.

All she could think about was the Circle. With Winn gone, they had lost their best hope of forcing the Alliance out of Bajoran territory. And Leeta couldn't help but wonder if it was her fault. For several days she had been worried, ever since Ziyal had confessed that their hired assassin had visited her. Leeta didn't understand how the mercenary had found Ziyal, when she had been disguised during their meeting. Why didn't the assassin contact Leeta, as she'd been told?

Leeta opened a channel to Ziyal. She was supposed to use it only during an emergency, and this certainly qualified. Ziyal was in the Ministry complex, close to Winn, so she would know what had happened.

It took some time for Ziyal to respond. Meanwhile, Leeta lifted the ground flyer from the Central Archives building and began to meander through the city, knowing it would be difficult to pinpoint her location. She felt absurdly paranoid, but she knew it was a protective mechanism to stop thinking about Adami. She would miss her . . . No matter how tired the First Minister was, she always took time to talk to Leeta. And the way she tended the orphans in her care was heartrending.

Leeta shook off the thought and concentrated on flying. But the reminders were everywhere as Bajorans poured onto the streets, their laments so loud she could hear them through the plasteel bubble of her ground flyer. They had lost their last, best hope . . .

Abruptly, Ziyal appeared on the tiny screen of her

communicator. She was holding it so close that only her eyes and the top of her head were visible. "Leeta, she's dead."

Ziyal's childish shock made it worse. "How? What happened?"

"We don't know! There was no disturbance, nobody came in." She looked over her shoulder, as if hiding in a closet. "I slipped out to talk to you, but Ministry security is still interviewing the staff."

"I heard it was Klingons," Leeta said, desperately trying not to think about what they were talking about.

"We found a Klingon knife," Ziyal stammered. "But it wasn't used. Her neck was broken—"

"Don't!" Leeta couldn't help but imagine it. Adami, the kindest person she had ever known, struck down so cruelly.

"I didn't tell security about you," Ziyal assured Leeta. "But I'm worried. I think I'm being followed."

Leeta knew the Circle was keeping watch over Ziyal. It was a precaution after the assassin had contacted her. Thank the prophets that Ziyal knew nothing about the Circle.

"Where are you?" Leeta asked.

"In the lavatory outside the courtyard."

That was a public spot in the Ministry. "Go back to work, and whatever you do, don't tell—"

The image of Ziyal wavered and slipped. She gasped out something that sounded like, "What are you doing?" The screen blurred as if moving too fast, then focused briefly on the ceiling.

Leeta quickly closed the channel and took the first

hard turn. That was not Ministry security. Ziyal's reaction had been too frightened.

Suddenly her paranoia was no longer abstract. Adami and now Ziyal . . . It seemed likely that she would be next.

She gunned the ground flyer out of the city, away from the government structures and employee housing, away from the business center and surrounding neighborhoods. There was a safe house she could go to in the nearby rural area, and from there the Circle would help her. It would be impossible for anyone to track her.

Leeta couldn't help thinking about her quarters high in the Archives tower. There were a few things there that she treasured: some holos of her family and her music and discs. Her new girlfriend would wonder what happened to her when she didn't show up tonight. Leeta hoped that no one would bother her—she didn't know anything about the Circle. Maybe later she could get a message to her girlfriend to reassure her that she was okay.

Leeta had friends and a life that she had risked by joining the Circle. But she had made this decision a long time ago. She would rather give up everything than be controlled by the Alliance. And now the day she had dreaded was finally here. She would have to give up everything.

Leeta had long since gotten muscle cramps in her neck from looking for pursuers. She had reached the winding outer roads, dotted by private compounds amid the rolling fields. The trees that marked the occasional crossroads were waving in the evening breeze.

She had slowed the ground flyer to conform to traffic regulations when she felt a tingle in the air.

Suddenly something appeared in front of the windshield, and she swerved. A person came flying through the windshield, face first, hitting the back of the passenger seat in a tangle of arms and legs.

Screaming, Leeta banked the flyer, but lost control of the skid. Still screaming, she was tossed into the air as the flyer bumped over a canal and ran into a hilly field. The nose hit the hillside with a jolt, and her head cracked against the bubble.

With several jarring bounces the flyer finally came to a stop.

Leeta was panting.

The person she had mowed down was trying to sit up in the passenger seat. Leeta, still gasping, touched the bubble in front of her. It was intact. Then she got a good look at the woman.

"You!" Leeta grabbed for her phaser pistol from under the seat. The hired assassin was leaning forward, shaking her head as if she had been hurt by the impact.

Leeta grabbed the back of her yellow hair and tilted her face up, holding the phaser under her chin. "I'm not going without a fight!" Leeta hissed.

Still holding the assassin tightly, she tried to see around them, expecting to be surrounded by a squadron of guards. But they were alone in the *mikos* field, a trail of crushed stalks left by their stalled flyer.

"How did you get here?" Leeta demanded.

The mercenary sounded exhausted. She no longer looked Bajoran, but had a smooth nose and yellow hair. But it was undoubtedly the same woman. "You would not believe me."

"Try me." Leeta felt breathless and panicked. None of this was right.

The assassin abruptly jerked her forward, thrusting her elbow into Leeta's stomach. She felt it happening, but didn't know how to stop it. In the next instant, Leeta was choking, unable to draw air into her lungs.

The mercenary calmly removed the phaser pistol from her spasmed hands. "Kira sent me through an ancient teleportation device."

Leeta fell forward, croaking out, "Traitor!"

"Now I will take you to Kira." The mercenary put something around her wrist.

Leeta struggled as hard as she could, kicking and punching, even though she couldn't breathe. But the mercenary was as unyielding as iron. Leeta was soon secured, with both her wrists locked behind her back and her ankles tied together. Lying sideways on the back seat of the flyer, Leeta watched as the woman grimly piloted the flyer back to the road, toward some unknown destination.

"Listen," Leeta urged desperately. "You don't have to work for Kira. You can't trust her. She'll hurt you just like she hurts everyone!"

The mercenary didn't bother to answer, piloting the ground flyer through the narrow back-country lanes. There was probably a space ship waiting up ahead to take them to Terok Nor.

"Do you want to see me tortured?" Leeta didn't care if her fear was obvious in her voice.

"No," the mercenary reluctantly admitted.

"I made a mistake," Leeta told her. "I know I

shouldn't have hired you to kill Kira. But you can't do this to me. You must have some heart."

The mercenary's jaw clenched. For a moment Leeta thought that she had managed to break through to her.

"Just let me go," Leeta urged. "You can always say you couldn't find me."

The mercenary hesitated, then firmly shook her head. "That is impossible. I must take you to Kira."

Leeta groaned, sure that she was heading to her death. But she knew one thing. . . .

But she knew one thing—she would not betray the Circle. No matter what else happened to her, as long as she protected her ideals, she would survive. She closed her eyes and then she could see Adami and Ziyal, both dead. Somewhere in the darkness waiting for her, Kira Nerys was laughing.

Chapter 21

KIRA NERYS RETURNED to Terok Nor after giving a heart-felt speech at Winn Adami's memorial service. The foster children had moaned and cried throughout, throwing her off a few times. Other than that, it had been perfect.

She was just in time to watch from the safety of the inner sanctum as Garak interrogated Leeta in the brig. The sound was muted, but the computer made audible the pertinent questions and answers.

Leeta writhed inside Garak's "interrogation booth," her body exposed to tiny lasers and beams of burning radiation. The Bajoran had a lovely body, and Kira hoped it would not be ruined before everything was revealed. But a bit of torment wasn't so bad . . . not after Leeta had plotted to kill her.

"Troi!" Leeta finally panted, her arms secured above her head. "The Intendant of Betazed . . . she wanted Winn to . . . replace Kira."

224

Garak looked up from the panel that controlled the barrage of electromagnetic waves. "Elaborate," he ordered.

"Winn didn't want to do it!" Leeta protested. Sweat slicked her bare skin. "But Troi's offer was too good . . . Anything to get rid of that monster!"

Kira glanced up and ordered, "Computer, mute any personal slurs the prisoner makes against me."

Garak twisted a dial. "So Winn told you and Tora Ziyal to hire an assassin?"

Leeta arched, grimacing. "Yes!"

Kira sat back. Leeta had corroborated the recording of Seven's discussion with Tora Ziyal. Garak continued to ask questions, but Leeta simply repeated the same thing, mingled with curses against the Intendant.

Meanwhile, all of Bajor was looking for Tora Ziyal. She had disappeared, making everyone believe that she had helped the assassin get into the Ministry. Kira was the only one who knew that Ziyal had disappeared because they had captured Leeta, her accomplice. She considered sending Seven through the Iconian portal to get her, but it suited her purpose to leave Ziyal running around. Soon she would be caught, and Winn's loyal public would see that she was properly punished. Right now, the Bajorans were up in arms against the Klingons and, because of Ziyal, the Cardassians as well. Kira's approval rating was rising higher with every passing hour.

She was pleased with the way things were going, especially with Seven. The Terran had expertly completed every task she had been given.

Kira turned to Marani. "I'll want a bath after this."

Marani silently inclined her head in obedience, just as Kira liked. The slave retreated to draw and scent a warm bath in the 'fresher.

Kira leaned forward and signaled Garak. He seemed reluctant to break from interrogating Leeta. *"Yes, Intendant?"*

Only because he desired to continue, Kira gestured dismissal at the limp, hanging form. "She's told us everything she knows."

"But, Intendant!" Garak protested, *"I've hardly begun! There may be others involved in this nefarious attempt on your life."*

Kira laughed at his distress. "You're enjoying this aren't you, Garak?"

Garak flushed a most interesting shade. *"As your security chief, it is my duty to protect you—"*

"Your duty is to obey me," Kira interrupted. When Garak closed his mouth, swallowing back his protests she demanded, "Unstrap that prisoner, clean her off, and deliver her to the cell in my quarters."

"Your quarters?" Garak asked in mock surprise.

Kira ignored him. She didn't really care about Garak or the prisoner. She wanted to find out more about Seven, her newest and most valuable acquisition. "Who was that mercenary who referred Seven to Leeta?"

Garak didn't need to consult the records of the interrogation. *"It was a Trill pilot called Jadzia."*

"I want you to find her."

Garak smirked. *"That shouldn't be too difficult. She's one of Sisko's crew members."*

"Benjamin!" The instant she let it slip, Kira regretted

letting Garak see her astonishment. But there was nothing she could do now.

"Yes. Didn't you know?" Garak pointedly drawled.

Kira narrowed her eyes. "I want that prisoner in my quarters immediately."

Grudgingly, Garak acknowledged, *"Yes, Overseer."*

Kira ordered Sisko to come to her quarters, then she kept him waiting while Marani bathed her. The last thing she had expected was for Sisko to be involved in this. She decided that if he knew about the assassination plot, he would die.

The scented bath and harmonious bell music soothed her nerves, agitated by the possibility of betrayal by one of her own servants. Benjamin, of all her Terrans, was given the most freedom. She delighted in his uninhibited enjoyment of life, his wide grin, and his passionate dark eyes. He was a big, dominant man who sometimes had to bend his head and submit to her. Why would she want to restrain a man like that?

Considering her favorite black skinsuit, Kira decided something more was needed. Marani tried several accesories until she found a black strap harness that fit snugly over her chest. Before Kira left her inner sanctum, she slipped a tiny hand phaser into one of her polished boots. She would put Ben down herself if he had betrayed her.

When Benjamin entered, his smile was as mocking as ever. "Why the wait? You know I like to watch you bathe . . ."

"Sit down," Kira said softly.

Sisko glanced around, but the chairs had been removed from the common room. He shrugged and got down, lying on one side and propping himself up with an elbow. "Nice rug," he told her, patting the crimson fibers. "Very soft."

He knew this was serious, but he refused to show fear. She liked that about him.

"Tell me about Jadzia," Kira ordered.

"Jadzia?" Sisko waved one hand. "She's a Trill pilot I met here on Terok Nor. Her ship was impounded for docking fees, so I hired her to replace a crewman. She went out on our last circuit . . . She sure knows her way around a warp ship."

"Quick work," Kira commented.

"Are you jealous?" Sisko asked, grinning.

Kira again ignored him. "What is her connection to Seven?"

Sisko shrugged. "Jadzia said she worked with her a few times. She tried to get Seven to help her when her ship was impounded, but Seven refused."

"Did she tell you what kind of job she recruited Seven for last time?"

"No. Why? What's going on?"

Kira stared at him for a few moments. "Maybe you know more than you're saying, Benjamin. Maybe I should let Garak talk to you and your new friend."

"Break your own toys?" He raised one brow at her. "What makes you think I'm lying?"

"Well, I have it on good authority that Jadzia recommended Seven to some Bajorans who wanted to kill me. We just finished interrogating one of them." There were sounds in the reception room of guards dragging some thing, and the sudden cry of a woman. "That must be her now."

Sisko pushed himself up to a sitting position, ready to rise. "Someone tried to kill you and Jadzia is involved?"

"That's what I'd like to know."

Sisko frowned, and Kira was reassured about his loyalty to her. But she didn't want him to know that.

Kira got down on one knee in front of him. "Tell me everything she told you."

Sisko seemed concerned. "Jadzia hasn't said much. But there's one thing that could be important. Jadzia thinks Seven might be Cardassian."

Kira was incensed. Could it be possible that Seven was a Cardassian in disguise? She had Seven immediately seized and scanned with a level-1 biodiagnostic unit. It took several hours to complete, so Kira continued to question Sisko and then Jadzia. Soon enough, Kira realized that Jadzia had no proof, only a hunch that Seven was Cardassian. That calmed her down considerably.

Garak wanted a crack at Jadzia to find out if she knew about the details of the contract. But according to Leeta, the Trill didn't know anything. Besides, it pleased her to deny Garak. He had gotten enough satisfaction from questioning Leeta. No reason to give him two beautiful women in one day.

When Serge brought the results from the biodiagnostic, Kira ordered everyone from the room so she could read it. Her relief to discover that Seven was Terran to her very bone marrow was almost more than she could admit. If she had been intimate with a Cardassian, she would never forgive herself.

Kira would have received Seven back into her inner sanctum with rejoicing except for one minor problem. According to the readouts, the Terran had a sophisticated implant in her head.

Kira went to Seven where she waited in her cabana room next to the pool. Seven was sitting on the low platform bed, holding on to the mat with both hands, looking up at Kira.

"Explain how you got that cranial implant," Kira ordered.

Seven took a deep breath. "When I was seven years old, my parents' scoutship crashed on a Cardassian colony. They were both killed. I was altered to appear Cardassian and was taken in by a local dignitary to replace a daughter who had recently died. A few years later, he was made a legate with Central Command. By then my foster parents had borne more children, and I was sent away to school on Cardassia Prime. I saw them only a few times after that until the family provided enough funds for me to leave Cardassian territory and set up as a mercenary. Apparently, I am an embarrassment to them."

"What about the implant?" Kira demanded.

"Everyone in the family received the implant when Ghemor was made legate. It will remain inert unless I am subjected to interrogation for secrets I may have overheard as part of the household."

Kira slowly smiled. "We could test that theory."

"I will do anything to prove my loyalty," Seven said doggedly. "I have killed for you, kidnapped for you . . . I will not stop at personal pain."

"So do you consider yourself Cardassian, having been raised by them?"

"No." Seven glanced down. "I'm not Cardassian. I'm not welcome on Cardassia Prime. I do not know what I am."

Kira knew that later she would have the computer thoroughly analyze this conversation to determine Seven's sincerity. Yet she already tended to believe her. It explained so much about her behavior and attitude. "I always thought you acted too proud for a Terran. But Cardassians have an insufferable conceit that you must have picked up."

"They taught me well," Seven hedged. "I will always be grateful they cared for me when I was young. However, they are highly xenophobic."

"Would you be willing to claim your Cardassian connections?"

Seven hesitated. "Ghemor would not be pleased. He is now a member of the Detapa Council. However, if it pleases *you*, I will do it."

Kira gave her an archly reproving look. "You become more interesting every day, Seven. But I'm not sure how many more secrets I can stand learning about you. You better tell me everything right now."

Seven raised her hands. "Now you know everything—more than anyone else. I'm alone, estranged from the few people who once cared about me. I survive as a mercenary pilot."

"I don't know about that," Kira murmured. "You seem destined for higher things."

Seven stood up and approached her. "I am destined for you."

Delighted as always by her brief declarations of affection, Kira stepped forward and took Seven in her arms, sealing the Terran's fate with a kiss. Kira began thinking how much she would revel in parading around a slave who had once been part of the Cardassian elite.

Kira tenderly lifted Seven's head. "We'll have to hurry, my dear. We have to get ready to go."

"Where?" Seven asked.

"To the former Terran Empire, of course! I must tour my domain, and I want you by my side." Kira didn't add that she needed to see Regent Worf and Deanna Troi together, to find out exactly how far this assassination plot had spread.

Seven merely nodded agreement, while Kira couldn't help thrilling to the idea of leaving Bajor. It was time she ventured out into the stars and tested her considerable power.

Star Trek: The Next Generation®

Star Trek: Deep Space Nine®

Star Trek: Voyager®

Star Trek®: New Frontier

Star Trek®: Invasion!

Star Trek®: Day of Honor

#1 • *Ancient Blood* • Diane Carey
#2 • *Armageddon Sky* • L.A. Graf
#3 • *Her Klingon Soul* • Michael Jan Friedman
#4 • *Treaty's Law* • Dean Wesley Smith & Kristine Kathryn Rusch
The Television Episode • Michael Jan Friedman
Day of Honor Omnibus • various

Star Trek®: The Captain's Table

#1 • *War Dragons* • L.A. Graf
#2 • *Dujonian's Hoard* • Michael Jan Friedman
#3 • *The Mist* • Dean Wesley Smith & Kristine Kathryn Rusch
#4 • *Fire Ship* • Diane Carey
#5 • *Once Burned* • Peter David
#6 • *Where Sea Meets Sky* • Jerry Oltion
The Captain's Table Omnibus • various

Star Trek®: The Dominion War

#1 • *Behind Enemy Lines* • John Vornholt
#2 • *Call to Arms...* • Diane Carey
#3 • *Tunnel Through the Stars* • John Vornholt
#4 • *...Sacrifice of Angels* • Diane Carey

Star Trek®: The Badlands

#1 • Susan Wright
#2 • Susan Wright

Star Trek®: Dark Passions

#1 • Susan Wright
#2 • Susan Wright

Star Trek® Books available in Trade Paperback

Omnibus Editions
    Invasion! Omnibus • various
    Day of Honor Omnibus • various
    The Captain's Table Omnibus • various
    Star Trek: Odyssey • William Shatner with Judith and Garfield
      Reeves-Stevens

Other Books

Legends of the Ferengi • Ira Steven Behr & Robert Hewitt Wolfe

Strange New Worlds, vols. I, II, and III • Dean Wesley Smith, ed.

Adventures in Time and Space • Mary P. Taylor

Captain Proton: Defender of the Earth • D.W. "Prof" Smith

New Worlds, New Civilizations • Michael Jan Friedman

The Lives of Dax • Marco Palmieri, ed.

The Klingon Hamlet • Wil'yam Shex'pir

Enterprise Logs • Carol Greenburg, ed.